Ralph Rokeby

Œconomia Rokebiorum

an account of the family of Rokeby written by Ralph Rokeby, one of the

Council of the North in the reign of queen Elizabeth

Ralph Rokeby

Œconomia Rokebiorum
*an account of the family of Rokeby written by Ralph Rokeby, one of the Council of
the North in the reign of queen Elizabeth*

ISBN/EAN: 9783337301873

Printed in Europe, USA, Canada, Australia, Japan

Cover: Foto ©Andreas Hilbeck / pixelio.de

More available books at **www.hansebooks.com**

Œconomia Rokebiorum

AN

ACCOUNT OF THE FAMILY OF

ROKEBY

Written by RALPH ROKEBY

One of the Council of the North in the Reign of QUEEN ELIZABETH

EDITED BY

A. W. CORNELIUS HALLEN, M.A.

F.S.A. (ScoL), Co. M. Scot. His. Soc.

(*Presented with the First Volume of* NORTHERN NOTES AND QUERIES.)

EDINBURGH: DAVID DOUGLAS

MDCCCLXXXVII

TO THE READER.

THE Transcript from which this version of *Œconomia* is printed was made in 1712 for Richard Boylston, Apothecary, Birmingham, who was the son of Henry Boylston of Lichfield, Gent., by his wife Rhoda, daughter of George Rokeby, who possessed a copy of the book. This MS. is now in the possession of John Charles Hallen, Esq., London, whose great-great-grandfather, John Clay Hallen, Gent., Attorney, Birmingham, married Sarah, only surviving child of Mr. Richard Boylston.

The Editor has to thank the Rev. H. R. Rokeby, R. Rookby, Esq., and J. Y. W. MacAlister, Esq., of the Leeds Library, for supplying some of the notes and various readings which are given in the Appendix.

Whittaker, in his *History of Richmond*, has printed a great part of the *Œconomia*, but does not state from what MS. it was taken.

The transcriber of Mr. Boylston's copy was evidently not a Latin scholar. It has been thought best to print his work exactly as he left it, *with all errors*.

The volume is a small quarto, and bound in calf; the writing is good. Dr. Zabdiel Boylston's work (see next page) is a printed volume of similar size and binding, and is valuable as containing the names of the persons inoculated by him in New England; with it is bound up Dr. Bradford's Sermon; the other volume mentioned in the list is lost.

He bareth Azure, Six Cross Crossetts fitchee
on a Chief Argent three Bezants;
Upon a Helmet a Lyon passant
holding a Crossett fitchee p͞r the
Name of Boylston.

---

1. Deconomia Rokebiorum.

2. History of the Lateral operation p͞r Douglass.

3. A Sermon (the Xtian Religion the occasion
   not the cause of Divisions', p͞r D. Bradford.

4. Cosin Zabdiel Boylstons History of Inocula-
   tion in New England.

In Nomine
Patri, et Filii, et
Spiritum.

Deconomia Rokebiorum

Written by RALPH ROKEBY, Jun
of Lincolns Inn.   To his very good
Nephews, Thomas, William, Ralph
Robert, and Ralph Rokebys.   1593.

1. Mine own Good Boyes and best Beloved Cozins; Seeing
that in these our times Honest Behaviour and fair Conditions are
so sore gone to Decay, that the old mens Proverb which they so
often and willingly mention is now verified ; (viz. oh it is not now
as it were in times past when we were young men,) and that
there is Such a General Declining from Good to Evil, and in Effect
to the worst of all, that we are almost descended to a General
Depravation of the Manners and Customs of our Life ; Since that
Such and So perrilous be the Times wherein your Lott is fall'n to
Step into this World, and withall that you are in that age wherein
Virtue in Gentle Minds, honest Dispositions, and patient of Labour
may begin to fasten take Root Bud and Blossom ; I have therefore thought Convenient to help you forward to desire and by
Good and Commendable means to deserve Honour or Honestie,
the fair and good reward of Vertue, with some few Arguments
and Examples ; and I did therefore now of Purpose Choose to do
it for that in these years being Allured with the praises of Commendable Actions to please and Delight your selves in well-doing
and also be affrighted with the Infamy of vicious Lewd and foul
Behaviour, to fear and Abhorr Shame and Dishonour as the Gates
of Hell ; thereby by God's Grace the Seeds of Vertue may now
take deep Root in you, and firme foot-hold and hereafter as Strong
plants may Augment and Increase as your witts and Courages
shall grow : for to use my Good old Uncle Dr. Rokeby his proverb
I will be plain with you S^r I care not a Rush for a young fellow of
a Gentle Kind that in his first youth feeleth not the needles or
stings of Honour to prickle him at the Heart and therefore suffereth
Himself to be Vanquished with these sweet pleasures to delight and
to be Glad to be praised for well-doing, and to have sorrow and be
shamed and to be Justly Blamed for Ill-doing ; for He that is not
passionated with the one of these or the other is of a vile Disposi-
tion, of a base and Cowardly Courage, and one who hath no will
to do well. And now (Good Boys) let my Advice sink into your
breasts when the vessell at the first seasoning taketh the Savour.
I will not pray you to Give Good Ear and heed to what I write
unto you for I know you love your Uncle, but I pray God Send my
Labours that Success that I conceive a Good Hope off : And I do
request and charge you all my nephews /^{s} Especially by name you
Ralph Rokeby, for you are a special part of my Charge, that you
first and principally call to your Remembrances continually that
you are Christians, and that you make your Earnest and Hearty
Dayly Prayers to God for His Assistance and Grace ; and then in
all Humility Study Daily some part of His Holy Scripture where
you shall Learn Steadfastly to believe in God the Father, the Son
and the Holy Ghost, Three persons and one God ; Almighty, all
Just, all Wise, and all Merciful ; as amongst all other things
appeared especially in that one thing, that when our Great Grand-
sires Adam and Eve had through Disobedience not only lost their

a

Blissful Earthly Paradice but also thrown themselves and all us their Posterity to the Bottomless pit of Hell there to have been Imprison'd from the Joyfull Sight of God and tormented with fire and Brimstone for Ever. The Eternal Mercy of God sent down God the Son the Second Person in Trinity to take our Nature upon him in all Humility and Obedience ; to Endure all the torments of this World, and Suffer Death for us ; yea God died to ransom us from Hell, from whence we could no way Escape, and thereby with his Everlasting Godhead in flesh in the form of a Servant he satisfied all that God's Justice could ask at our Hands, being himself that made this Satisfaction, all just, all perfect God and Man, to be praised and Blessed for Ever ; Oh ! the Incomprehensibleness and Inaccessibleness of God ! His Wisdom and Goodness ; Godhead Could not Suffer, Manhood could not Satisfie God and Man ; the person Jesus Christ did both, and to that end united both those natures into one Essence or Person ; and that day His omnipotencie and Almightyness Shined forth by his own Power he praised himself again out of the Bodies of Death where He overcame Death and the Divill, and threw down the Gates of Hell; so that they cannot any Longer press down those that be of his Flock ; and finally he left up Himself thither ; where he first Descended, and whence he shall once come again at the Sound of the Last Trump, to Judge both the Quick and the Dead, and thereby hath opened to us the Gate of Everlasting Life ; the which he /[a] hath Given and Bequeathed us for a Legacy by his Last Will and Testament written in his Apostles and Prophets in the Books of the two Testaments ; and hath sealed the same Covenant and Bequest by his Precious Blood upon the Cross, and Even (as I may say) branded the same upon our Flesh by the Sacraments of Baptism, and of his Holy Supper ; by the which he giveth himself to us and taketh us to Him; if we come to it with an Assured Faith, Lowly Mind, and True Repentance : The which work of Incomprehensible pitty that the Holy Trinity hath done for us to this End, that we should Honour and Love him our Good God above all, and our neighbour as our selves. This believed and followed I doubt not will be a Sound Root whereout Moral Vertue will Spring and flow to the Beautifying your Civil Lives, and yet I exhort you not only to found your Lives on my Speeches, but upon Holy Prayers, poured forth for the assistance of God's Holy Spirit, and Examination and Conferrence with the Holy Scriptures ; which you must Dayly and hourly Early and Late Read with Devout Zealous and Hearty Prayers ; to read them Reverently, understand them Truly, and Live after them Religiously ; then to Receive it from your Good Uncle. And for your further Instruction in the way and fear of God make your Continual repair to Godly Sermons without the which you shal neither make Good Beginning nor Ending for Fides per Auditum et quomodo invocabunt eum, in quem non crediderunt qumodo Credent vi, Quem non Audierunt quomodo audient, sine praedicante, and the beginning of wisdom is the fear of the Lord, which God grant us all, Amen. /⁴ A second Admonition wherewith I would perswade you to an Even and Upright Course of Life, is that you shall continually in all your doings have in remembrance that (Thanks to God) you are Gentlemen, who how they must be Quallified, and how they must behave themselves, read Solomon's Proverbs, his Wisdom, Ecclesiasticus, Ecclesiastes, Tullies Offices, Cant. Baltazzar, Castillio of the Courtier and how to furnish them to serve their King and Country in peace and Warrs read Polibius, Cornelius Tacitus, Plutarch's Lives, Philip de Comines, the Great Counsellor of State to Lewis the Eleventh, the French king, and the valiant Charles Duke of Burgundy ; Francis Guiccardine, the Sweet Frenchman of Geneva who writ the Antient Machiavell Dedicated to Mr. Francis Hastings, and Edward Bacon, and Lambert Daneus, his Aphorismata Politica ; and this rank of Gentlemen your Ancestors have kept since the Norman Conquest ; your name and Blood is from the Saxons as I think ; Howbeit to convey your Pedigree by Just Descents, the negligence and Injury of former times hath denied any sure and certain proofs but the Town of Rokeby upon Greta and Hartley Castle now in the Tenure of Sʳ Simon Musgrave Kᵗ were yoʳ ancestors antient dwellings, and with the same Sʳ. Simon are also to be found, I do think some proofs and monuments of the Antiquity of your Family ; I am sure there is a Star in the Demaynes of Hartley yet called Rokeby's Star and so my good Cousin Richard Musgrave told me : as also I have credibly heard that there is in a Record of a Tryall of a Coat Armes remaining in the custody of the /⁵ Lord Scroope of Bolton ; some remembrance of the Antiquity of our House, for they say that his Coat Armes (in Richard the seconds time) being Litigious betwixt him and Carmeno of Devonshire, for that they both bare the same Coat arms without Difference, (a Thing Unlaw-full amongst Christians) was tryed by Gentlemen, then known to be of antient family whereof an Ancestor of yours was one, and that was then Antient (is now a majore) as the Logicians argueth. The House of Rokeby was burned (as I have heard it said) by the Scots in the time of K Edward the Second, whereoff now only remaineth the Chappel and Dow-Coates, and the old Groundwork of the Walls, whereupon your Ancestors haveing married Mansfield his Daughter and heir of Morton by the Perswasion, (I Ghess) either of an Exceeding good Wife whom he dearly Loved, or else of an Extream evil one, of whom he stood greatly in fear ; or happily enticed by the Strength and Pleasure of the Scite, then which I know few more answerable to my Liking ; Left the old Seat of the House at Rokeby and Builded upon the knap of the Hill, within two flight Shoots of the old House, and within a Roveing Shot of the Meeting of the two rivers Tease and Greta, where yet till this Day (God be thanked) Continueth the House of

our whole Family and Parentage, the Antient Arms and Ensigns
of Honour, which our Ancestors have Continually borne are Argent,
a Chiveron Sable betwixt three Rooks proper, the which you
partake every one according to his Birth, which you Difference as
you do; Also the Blood and Arms of Mansfield of Morton, the
Lord Scroop of Upshall, /⁶ Conygers alias Conyers, Bowes, Darby,
Laughton of Walton in Lancashire, Strother of Strode in Northumberland, Holmes of Paul Holme in Yorkshire, Wastnes of Hayden
in Nottinghamshire, and Elland of Hull, by all the which by the
Laws of Armes you are Gentlemen in blood in your Coat Armes
which are of antient bearing, you are to acknowledg thankfully to
God, that it consisteth of Mettle and Colour most fair and Honourable, Ordinary and a Charge proper; All good notes in Armory
to Disclose an Advancement only for Vertue.

And for the Continuance of the same Gentle Blood to descend
from you to your Children which God may Lend you, lest happily
ungentle manners in you, Should make an alteration and Corruption
of the Blood, and stop those Good fountains that they Cannot besprinkle your Children; I will propound to you as a pattern to
follow, no Strange nor far fetcht Stories but some of Your own
Ancestors, who have born Light and Credit in the Countrie, and
thereby gave the History of their time Some matter to write of
their Good and Honourable proceedings. To the which writers
You and we all must acknowledge ourselves greatly bounden, for
even as our Parents have got and left us to Serve our King and
Country, So those good and Learned men in their painfull Labours
and writings, Commending to fame and history our ancestors well-
doings, teach us in the footsteps of our forefathers vertues, how we
ought to serve the same our King and Country, and therefore I will
recite their Names and Authority as the Sequell and Suit of Time
brought them forth; And our first benefactor that I know that
way is found in a Chronicle Called Scala Chronica reported by Mr.
John Leland to be translated out of French /⁷ into English by one
of the Grayes of Northumberland, for that they give the Ladder
in their Crest; who reporteth that an army of Scots about the first
year of Edward the 3d as I find by other Chronicles, haveing
Invaded this Land with Sword and fire; Bellows and Handmaids
of Destruction; your Ancestor Sʳ Thomas Rokeby brought him
and his army So as he intrapped the Scots at Stanhope park, and
had them all at his mercy, the King himself and his Army being
out of all Danger; for which he was by the same Worthy King
Rewarded with one Hundred pound Land by the Year parcell of
which Land was the Mannor of Pouls Gray alias Gray poulen in
Kent; Sold by the same Sʳ Thom to the Lord Scroop of Upsall,
and now being in the Hands of one hunt of London, a Sopeseller,
of the which Covenants from him to the Lord Scroop, I myself
have seen the Charters under our Seal of Arms, dated the 4th of
Edward the 3d, to my best remembrance reciting the Kings grant.

Ex rotulo Patentium de Anno 1°
Regni Regis Edward 3ᵈ

Edwardus Dei Gratia Rex Angliae, Dominus Hyberniae & Dux
Aquitainiae, omnibus ad Quos presentes litera pervenerint. Salu-
tem Sciatis quod cum nuper in partibus borealibus cum exercutu
nostro fuimus proclamari facerimus, quod ille qui nos perdueret ad
nisum immicorum nostiorum, ubi eos appropinquare possemus
super terra Sicca, pro facto ab eis habendo, sibi faceremus habere
Centum libratas Terrae per Annum ad terminum vitae Suae et
dilectus, et. Fidelis noster, Thomas de Rokeby nos perduxerit ad
visum inimocorum nostrorum praedictorum in Loco /ᵃ duro, et
Sicco, juxt proclamationem praedictum, nos volentes Proclamationem illam, et promissionem nostram ad impleri, concessimus
eidem, Thomae, Centum Libris per Annum percipiendas ad
Sciacarium nostrum ad Terminos Sancti Michaelis & Pascha per
Equalis portiones, quousq dicto Thomae Providerimus, de Centum
Libratis Terra per Annum habendis ad Terminum vitae Suae, In
cujus rei Testimonium has Literas nostras fieri facimus patentes,
Tester Meipso apud Lincolinam Vicessimo Octavo die Septembris
Anno Regni 1°.

But the Same Army of Scots the which your Ancestor gave to
the King and his Country as Fettered prisoners, a wicked man of
the King's Privy Councel, and Somewhat too familiarly acquainted
with the Queen-Mother ; as Some say Sʳ Mortimer Earl of March
and Ulster, let them go safe, and free out of the Kings danger for
money, and also delivered unto them the great Charta Regina,
wherein the Homage and Obedience of the Scottish Kings to the
Kings of England, were extant; for the which afterwards he
worthily Lost his Head. Loe my lads the good success of your
Ancestors well doing, and Dutiful Service to his prince and
Countrie, and acknowledge the Largess and Magnanimity of that
Worthy and famous King, and by the way mark well the just and
due Hire of Treachery, and Treason, in the Miserable end of that
great person Mortimer ; and Learn out of this History how greatly
beneficial it may be to a Soldier to know all ways and Passages.
/ᵖ I read also of this our Ancestor collected by Mr. John Leland,
out of a Chronicle of William Packington, Treasurer to Prince
Edward, Son to Edward the 3d, his Household in Gascoyne, who
writ a Chronicle in French, from the ninth year of King John of
England unto his Time ; and dedicated it to his Lord Prince
Edward ; that about the 20th year of the same King Edward the
3d, by the means of Philip Unlois [*sic*], King of France, David
King of Scots entered into the north Marches, Spoyling and Burn-
ing ; and took by York the Pile of Lyddel, and caused the noble
Knight Sʳ Walter Selbie, Captain of it to be slain before his face,
not suffering so much as to make his Confession ; and after he
came to the Coast of Durham, and lay there at a place called Bear
park, a Mannor of the Priors of Durham, set in a Park, and thither

resorted many of the Country about, who Compounded with him
to spare their Lands and Mannors ; Then William Souch, Arch
Bishop of York, the Count of Angou, Monsieur John de Mount-
bray, Monsieur Henry de Pierce, Monsieur Ralph de Nevill,
Monsieur Ralph de Hastings, Monsieur Thomas de Rokeby, the
Sheriff of Yorkshire, and other Knights and good men of Worth,
marched toward ye Scots, and first Lay in Auckland park, and in
the morning encountered with Sr William Douglass, killing of his
Army 200 men, but he with much ado Escaped to Bear park
declaring the comming of the English Host; whereupon King
David Issued out, and fought upon a Moore near Durham and
there was taken Prisoner, and Sr William Douglas with him, the
Count of Meneth, and the Count of Fife, and a great number of
the Commons of Scotland was Slain, the /[10] King (because he was
wounded in the Face) was carried to Werk and so brought to
London.   The third man that hath befriended us with the mention
of our Ancestors was a reporter of the Laws, that reported that
Ancient Law Book, called the Book of Assigns, in the 22d year
of that book, the which Reporteth the Judgment of the Laws at
the Assizes holden ye same year, in the 49 number of Pleas there,
and in the 95 Plea on the 97 Leaf, it is recorded that John Hill of
Flowath was Indicted and Condemned of High Treason before
Sr Thomas Rokeby K^t then Sherriff of Yorkshire, for slaying
Adam Walton the Kings Ambassador, going on the dispatch of the
Kings affairs; and that the Prior of St Leonard in York that claimed
the goods of men any ways condemned, could not by that general
grant, have the Goods of an High Traytor.   It appeareth there
also that Sr Henry Viscie, was there Indicted before him of Felony
in the 9th year of King Edw. the 3d.   You must forth of the
records gather these Instructions ; *Frist,* that it is High Treason
to kill the King's Ambassador, for that he representeth the Kings
Royal Person in Majesty.   2, That the Kings grant must be
expounded in a Beneficiall Construction for his Majestie ; when he
giveth away anything growing to him by the Prerogative of the
crown of England, and nothing passeth from him, ex ui Litaere
because he is the Head of the Commonwealth, Common Laws,
Common Peace ; and that therefore especial words, apt for every
particular, be needful in Conveyances from the King in that Case;
and *Thirdly* that such Magistrates as Sr Thomas was must assist
the King and Country to condemn an /[11] Hang up Thieves and
Traytors : Mr. Raphael Hollingshead that of Late hath writ the
Great Chronicle, and hath this History of Sr Thomas Rokeby (the
same man still I think) that he was Lord Justice in Ireland, in the
same King Edward 3d time, in the 29th year of his Raign, and that
once being Upbraided by one Somwhat too Curious (as it Seemeth)
for that eating his meat upon a Wooden Dish, and Drinking in a
wooden Cup, he answered my Friend this is paid for, and was well
gotten, assuredly a happy wooden Dish, whereby a Golden mind was

So well Declared ; to abhorr Delicacy and Excess ; to account of wood well gotten, more than of Gold Scraped together by Evil and undue means; to Esteem whatsoever he had if he had paid for it, and run not therefore into poor mens Debts, (precious) and finally, that chose rather to Adorn his place of Majestie under his Prince with Just and True dealing, than his own Private house with Gold and Precious moveables. Raphael Hollingshead, his words, fol. 63d be these : viz., After Maurice Fitz Thomas Earle of Desmond, Lord Justice of Ireland succeeded in that room Thomas de Rokeby, a Knight Sincere and Upright of Conscience who being Controuled that he was served in Treene cups Answer'd these homely cups pay Truly for what they contain I rather drink out of Treen Cups and pay Gold and Silver then Drink out of Gold and make Wooden payment ; O my good Boys ! forget not this good and Golden Speech, and be ashamed whilst you Live once to make such a Worthy Gentleman groan in his Grave at any of your misdemeanours. I cannot tell how this good man Ended his Life, by reason of the Long Interposition of Times since Edw 3d his Raign and us, /12 and also by the Desolation of Egleston Abby wher the monuments of most of your Ancestors burials were ; but this one thing I presume, that he died well, and that his Soul now enjoyeth the Bliss of Heaven, and his Bones and Ashes peace in the Earth, for all men ought to Judge to so good a Life a Blessed Death ; and now you and I kissing the memory of this Arch Peer of our Family will Humbly take our Leaves of Sr Thomas Rokeby, and peruse by the way Mr. Halls Chronicle in the Reign of King Henry the fourth ; where you shall find that Sr Ralph Rokeby, being Sheriff of Yorkshire only with the power of his Country, without staying for Assistance of the Kings power, Incountered in the field an Army of Scots at Brammam Moore, who under the Conduct of the Earls of Northumberland and March, had made a Sudden Invasion into the Country ; Vanquisht them, took their Captains Prisoners, and Executed the Earl of Northumberland. I must here tell you that I ghess, he did thus adventerously hazzard this onset, because the Spoiling Enemy of Necessity required presently to be affronted and Suppresed ; the which I touch to this purpose, for that I am sure some wary Worldly men will carp at his forward proceeding, as too heady, Savouring of rashness ; and Indeed some say it had Like to have cost your Ancestor Sr Ralph his Headpiece, and a common fame is in our parts, that much of his Lands was seized for his Contempt, in fighting the Enemy without a Commission ; but in my opinion the just anger of a Captain in Chief against an Enemy, Traytor to his King /13 and who had Burned and spoyled all the North to Brammam Moore, being all to be chafed with the heat of the Battle that he freshly came from, might worthily inflame a mind full of magnanimity, even to kill that Capital Enemy, in whose death Lay the End and Consummation of his victory, and the Quiet and Good of his King and Native Country So it were not done Cruelly in Cold Blood, and I could not see how he could have been Excused of Remiss dealing, Cowardize and Unlawfull and evil Government if he had Stayed in Sending to the King for Soldiers, till the Barbarous Enemy had Spoiled, Wasted, the Land ; Stay is Indeed a worthy property in a General of an Army, and a Battle is not to be fought and Hazzarded but upon most Urgent occasions ; but without Extremities upon the Sudden are Sometimes to be prevented or else never ; and necessity hath neith Law nor Limits ; And whiles our Native Country burneth, to Consult what to do when the Enemy may be Resisted with force, is neither (in mine opinion) base Cowardise, nor Treachery and Treason : Mr. Lelands reporteth this History out of a Chronicle of Malmsbury Abby, called Eulogium Historiarum, autore Monacho ejusdem loci Sed incerti nominis. Which says that the Nobles of Scotland brought the Earl of Northumberland, the Lord Bardolph, and the Abbott of Hales to Tweed water, bidding them now proceed, (you have England wth you), and alleaged that about Tadcaster The Sherriff of Yorkshire killed him, (but not naming your ancestor) but Hall and the Mirrour of Magistrates name him and therefore Youths if ever you prove Captains /[14] and Leaders of Men never adventure a Battle rashly upon Light occasion, nor in Extremity, Stand too Long in terms of Advice and Consultation ; but with a Lusty courage Set upon the Enemies of your King and Country, like English men, and right Heirs of those two worthy persons your ancestors ; of whom both you and I will take our Leaves, Thanking our God who appointed them to Supply those Honourable places and Estates ; and in them to Supply, and do their Prince and Country Good Service ; We cannot chose but think of them to our Good and great joy and Comfort, Speak of them with reverence and Imitate their Good with all Diligence. I find no more of our Name in English History Save only this in Lincolns-Inn Black book, that in the Reigns of King Henry the 6th, Henry the 7th, Henry 8th, Edward the 6, Queen Mary and our Sovereign Lady· Elizabeth's time, there hath been Continually a Rokeby, Lawyer and Governour of the Bench of that House ; and ever in Effect, from the Counsell in the North errected, there hath one or more of our name Served in that place ; but I hear say there is some more of our Family to be found in the Scottish History about the affairs of Dunbretton Town, but what it is, or in what time, I know not, nor can have Convenient Leisure to Search for it. Parson Blackwood the Scottish Chaplain to the Lord Gro, of Shrewsbury, recited me once a piece of old Scottish Song, whereby it was mention'd that William Wallis, the great Deliverer of the Scots from the English, should at Dunbretton have been brought up under a Capt. Rokeby, then of that peice, and as he walked upon the /[15] Cliff, should thrust him on the Sudden into the Sea, and thereby have gotten that hold ; which was about the 33d of Edward 1st or before ; and thus Leaving our Ancestors of Record we must also leave with them the Chronicles, and Copy down unwritten Stories, the which have yet the Testimonie of Later times, and the fresh memory of men yet alive, for their Warrant and Credit; of whom I have Learned that in King Henry the Seventh his Reign, one Ralph Rokeby Esq., was owner of Morton, who by report Lived well and Honestly in his Calling: and I guess, that this was he that Deceived the Friers of Richmond with his Selling Swine, of which a Jargon was made, and I have heard the Beginning of a Rude Rhime in these Words,

> The men that will of Aunters meane
> That Lately in this Land hath bene,
>   Of one I will you tell ;
> Of a Sew at was Sea Strange
> Alas at ever She lived Sea Lange,
>   For Fell folke did She wheell.
> She was maire then other three,
> The Griestlest Beast at ever might be,
>   Her Head was great and Graye :
> She was bred in Rokeby Wood,
> There was few that thither Yode
>   That came on live away.
> Her walk was End lange Greta Side,
> There was bien that Durst her bide
>   That was fro Heaven to Hell :
> Nor never man that had that Might,
> That ever Durst come in her Sight
>   Her force it was Sea fell. /[16]
> Ralph of Rokeby with full good will,
> The friers of Richmond gave her till
>   Full well to gar them faire ;
> Frier Middleton by his Name
> He was Sent to fetch her hame
>   At rued him Since full Sore.
> With him took he Wight men twoe
> Paterdale was one of thoe,
>   That ever was Brim as Bear :
> And well durst Strike with Sword or knife,
> And feight full Manfully for his Life
>   What time at Nusts weare.
> These three ment at Gods wil,
> This wicked Sow, while they came till,
>   Liggand under a Tree :
> Rugge and Rusty was her haire,
> Sho rase up with a fellen faire
>   To fright again the Three.
> Sho who was So griesley for to meete ;
> Sho rase the Earth up with her feete,
>   The Bark came fro the Tree :
> When Fryer Middleto her Saughe,
> Weet ye well he might not Laughe,
>   Full Earnestly Look't hee.
> These men of awnters that was Sea wight
> They bound them bowdly to the fight
>   And Strake at her full Seare :
> Until a Kilne they gart her flee

Note : that these verses are Writ and Spelt as the original Copy.

Wald God send them the Victory,
  I walde ask him no meare.
The Sew was in the Kiln-hole,
As they were on the balks abow,
  For hurting of their feet : /[17]
They were Sea assaulted with this Sew,
That amang them There was a Stallworth Stew
  The Kilne began to reeke ;
Durst no man neigh her with his Hand,
But put a Reape down with his Wand,
  And haltered her full meet.
The hurled her forth against her will,
Whiles they coome unto a Hill
  A little fro the Street :
And there She made them Such a fraye,
As if the Should to Domesday,
  The Tharrow it never forget,
She braded up on every Side,
And ran on them gapeing full wide,
  For nothing would She lett :
She gave Such braides that the brand,
That Paterdale had in his Hand
  He might not hold his feet.
She chaufed them to and fro,
That Weight men never was So woe
  Their measure was not meet :
Sho bound her boldly to abide,
To Paterdale Sho came aside
  With many a Hedious Yell :
Sho gaped Soe wide and cried Sea hee
The Frier Said I conjure thee
  Thou art a fiend of Hell ;
Thou art come hither for Some Traine
I.conjure thee to go againe
  Where thou was wont to Dwell.
He Signed him with Cross and Creed,
Took forth a Book began to read
  On St Johans Gospell ; /[18]
The Sew Sho would not Latin heare,
But only Noked at the Fryer,
  That blenched at his Blee :
And when Sho would have tane her hould
The Fryer leaped as Jesus would,
  And Brauld him with a Tree.
Sho was as brim as any Beare,
For all their Might to Labour were
  To them it was no boote :
Upon Trees and busks as by her Stood,
She venged her as Sho was Wood,
  And rave them up by Root.
He said alas that I was Frier
And I shall be Rug'd in Sunder here
  Hard is my Destinye :
Wist mee brethren in this houre
That I was Set in such a Stowre
  Yet walde they prayed for me.
This wicked beast that wrought this woe
Took the rape fro the other twoe,
  And then they fled all three :

They fled away by Watling Streete
They had no Succour but their feete,
   It was the more Pitty.
The fielde was both Lost and Won,
The Sew went hame again full soon,
   To Morton on the Greene,
When Ralph of Rokeby Saw the rape,
He wist at there had been Debate,
   Where at the Sew had beene.
He bad them Stand out of her way
For Sho had had a Sudden Fraye
   I saw her never So keen :
Some new things Shall we hear
Of her and Middleton the Frier
   Some Battle there hath been. /[19]
But all that Served him for naught,
Had not the better Succor Sought,
   They were ferd therefore Loe :
Then Mrs. Rokeby came anone,
And fall her brought Sho Meat full Soone
   The Sew came her unto.
And gafe her meat upon the Floor,
And noy Sho did byer no more.
   When Frier Middleto came home,
His brethren was full faine ilke one
   And Thanked God for his Life :
He tould them all unto the End
How he had foughten with a Fiend
   And Lived in Mickle Strife.
Then the Letters was well made,
Bands bond with Seales brade,
   As deeds of Armes Should bee :
These men of Armes at was Sea weight,
With Armour and with brands bright
   They went this Sew to See ;
Sho made on them Sike a rerde
That for her they were Sore aferd
   And almost bound to flee.
Sho came roveing them againe
That Saw the Bastard Son of Spaine,
   He braided out his Brand :
Full Spightfully at her he Strake,
For all the force at he could make,
   Sho gat Sword forth of his hand.
And rave in Sunder half his Shield,
And bare him backward in the Field ;
   He might not her gaynstand :
Sho would have riven his privy geare,
But Gilbert with his Sword of weare
   He strake at her fast then : /[20]
On her Shoulder till Sho held his Sword,
Then was good Gilbert sare afferd,
   When the blade brake in Strange.
Since in his Hand he hath her Tane
Sho took him by the Shoulder beane
   And held her hold full fast,
He Straw so Stiffely in that Stoure,
That through all his rich armore,
   The Blood ran out at Last.

Then Gilbert grieved was Sea Seare,
That he rave off both Hide and Hayre
  The flesh came fro the Beane :
And all with force he felled her there,
And wan her worthily in weare,
  And band him alone.
An Kest her on a Horse Sea hee
In two Panzers well made of Tree,
  And to Richmond anone he brought her :
Now when they Saw her come,
They Sang merrily Te Deum
  The Fryers every day :
They thanked God and S⁺ Francis,
As they had won the Beast of Prise
  And never a man was Slain.
We gave her battle half the Day,
And Sichin was fain to flee away
  For saveing out our Life :
And Paterdale would never blin ;
But as fast as he could Run
  Till he came to his wife.
The Warden Said I am full woe,
That ever ye Should be tormented Soe,
  But had wee with zou beene ; /²¹
Had we been there your brethren all,
We Should have gart the Warle fall,
  That wrought you all this deene.
Frier Middleton Sayd Soone nay,
In faith ye would have fled away
  When most mister had been :
You will Speike words at haime,
A man would ding ye every ilke ;
  And it be as I weene.
He lookt So griesly all the nighte,
The warden sayde you man will fighte,
  If ye Say out but good :
Zoe ghest hath grieved him Sea Sare,
Hold your Tongue and Speake noe mare,
  He looks as he were woode.
The warden waged on the morne
Two boldest men that ever was borne,
  I ween and ere Shall bee :
The one was Gilbert Griffins Son,
Full mickle worship has he won,
  Both by Land and Sea.
The other was a Bastard Son of Spaine,
Namde Sarazin hath he Slaine,
  His Diat hath gart the Die.
These two men the battle undertooke,
Against the Sew as Sayth the booke,
  And Sealed Securelye.
That they Should boldly bide and fight,
And Scomfit her in maine and might,
The warden Sealed to them againe,
And Said if ye in field be slayne,
  This condition make I /²²
Wee Shall for you Pray, Sing and reade
Till Domsday with hartie Speed,
  With all our Progeny.

There did never man yet more manly,
Knight Marcus nor yet Sir Guye
　　More lothe of Lowth Rime :
If ye will any mare of this,
In the Fryers of Richmond written it is,
　　In parchment Good and fine :
And how Fryer Middleton at was sea lend
At Greta Bridge Conjured a fiende
　　In likeness of a Swine.
It is well known to many a man,
That Fryer Theobald was warden then,
　　Blest both far and neere,
All that for Solace List this to hear
And him that made the Rime.
Ralph Rokeby with full good will,
The Fryer of Richmond he gave her till,
　　This Sew to mend their fare :
Fryer Middleton by his name,
Would needs bring the fat Sew haime
　　That rewed him Since full Sare.

Be like the Fryer boasting of his manhood, never bid the Shame
in all his Life but once, and that was the Sow at Morton. This
Song old William Luther Sᵣ Edmond Maulivery his man held so
rare a Record that he would not teach it to his Son, for fear his
Skill in Antiquity Should thereby be blemished with this Jargon.
I have seen in an antient written hand before print was known a
Comment of Some Silly Paraphrasting Frier of Newburgh, as I
guess, for Sᵣ Wᵐ Bellasis owner thereoff gave it me, /²³ Comparing
the Sow to the Sow Lechery, and Mᵣ Rokeby to the Kirk that
would not have the Sow ; and Concluded that the Good father
Friers were felloniously bitten with the Sew. The same Ralph
Rokeby had to his Brothers, Wᵐ Rokeby Esqᵣ an Atturney at
Law, and Justice of Peace, and one who married Grace, one of the
Daughters of Fith-Harris in Mansfield ; and by her had Ralph
Rokeby Esqᵣ his Eldest Son, Justice of the Peace. William
Rokeby Clerk Arch-deacon of Cleaveland, and Judg of one of ye
Spritual Courts of York. And Lawrence Rokeby, Gent. and
Merchant of Newcastle upon Tine. Ralph the Son of William had
Issue Robert Rokeby Esqᵣ owner of Mask who Livith at this time
(being 1593) I thank God, an honest and upright Gentleman.
William, another Son of the Same William Dyed without Issue.
Lawrence another of Williams Sons had Issue, and John Rokeby
now dwelling at Newcastle upon Tine. Rokeby Eldest of Ralph
of Mask, had by Salven his wife, Issue 4 Sons, Ralph, Christopher,
Robert and 　　　　　[sic] & Three Daughters Ellen, Margret
and Joane. Ralph the Eldest is married to 　　　　[sic] and
now Dwelleth at Mansfield, and this is the Pedigree of the House and
Branch of Mask, and Newcastle, whom God by Learning, Mer-
chandize, honest Lives and Good Dealing hath advanced to a
worˡˡ abillity, and place of Credit in our Country.
　/²⁴ In the Same K Hen 7ᵗʰᵉ time must I also derive forth of the

House of Morton, the Branch of Staningford and of Clowbeck, another family of our name that thanks be to God, liveth in honest whole Credit in the Country, able to defend the force of their Foes, and befriend their friends for the old Ralph Rokeby of Morton had also another Brother named James Rokeby Esqr one of the Auditors of the Marquiss of Northampton ; and after that of King Henry 8th and one of the Court of the Augmentation of his Revenues. This James builded by the Perswasion of his Second wife, the House of Weston, where Mr Vavasour Liveth upon Wharf Bank ; He had Issue Martin Rokeby, his Eldest Son, Deceased ; and James his Youngest Son, now owner of Staningforth, by Jane the Daughter of Sr William Middleton of Stockeld K^t who Liveth at this Day, worthy his good Ancestors to our Credit and his Comfort. This James the younger Son of James Rokeby the Auditor, he Married the Daughter of   [sic] Gascoign of Caley, by whom he hath Issue, Anthony, Thomas, Jane and Elizabeth ; Anthony first married the Daughter of Wm Sutton of Aram near Newark Esqr by whom he had Issue, Henry a Spanish Merchant Dyed beyond Sea. By his Second Wife Mary the Daughter of James Abney of Wilsley in Derbyshire near Ashby-de-la-Zouch ; had Issue, George, Thomas, Fulk, Anthony ; and five Daughters, Frances, Margret, Elizabeth, Ann and Eleanor ; George the Eldest Son /[25] of Anthony married Grace the Daughter of Tho : Underwood of   [sic] and hath Issue, John, George, James, Thomas, Ralph, and three Daughters Grace, Rhode and Sarah, whom I pray God So Guide and Direct, by the powerfull assistance of his Holy Spirit, that following the vertue of their Worthy Ancestors, they may Glorifie God in this World, and be Glorified of God in the World to come.

Thomas Rokeby, Second Son of Anthony Rokeby of Staning-ford, Clark and Master of Arts ; is now Vicar of Norwell in Nottingham-Shire, by Donation of Gervace lee Esq Husband of Eleanor Rokeby, youngest Daughter of Anthony Rokeby : And the Said Thomas Rokeby is also Parson of Warmsworth in York-shire, near Doncaster, by Donation of Thomas Bossevillc of Edlington Esq. This Thomas Rokeby hath at his own proper Costs and Charges bestowed the best part of two-hundred Pounds in the repairing the Mention Houses belonging to those two Churches of Norwell and Warnsworth ; having builded that of Warmsworth from the very Ground ; Dedicating himself and all that he hath to the Honour of God, and the Good of Gods Church ; of whom I will say no more but this, that as he lives in the fear of God So at the last he may Dye in Gods favour, and Receive that Blessing promised to all those that fear the Lord, Amen.

                                                                    [sic]
Fulk Rokeby the 3^d Son of Anthony Rokeby of Staningford, /[26]

Anthony Rokeby the 4th Son of Anthony Rokeby of Staningford liveth at Thorgarten in Nott. and hath married the Daughter of John Grundie of Thorgarten; by whom he hath Issue, William Rokeby, an Infant, whom I pray God to bless, that as he Grows in Years, So he may grow in Grace with God, and favour with all Men.

And Since the aforesaid Anthony Rokeby hath Anthony, George, Godfry, and Two Daughters Mary and

[sic]

Martin the Eldest Brother had Issue Tho Rokeby his Eldest Son, and James his Youngest Son, two honest poor Gent. whom we must all Do our best to Comfort and Relieve. He hath Issue also John Rokeby, Slain in Flanders, and Cuthbert, and Anthony; and thus Much of the House and Family of Stanningforth.

In the Same K Hen 7th and part of K Hen 8th Reign the Same old Ralph Rokeby lived at Morton, whose House I will Leave for a Time, and return my Speech towards the House of Sandal near Doncaster; of the which House and Branch your Mothers were two Daughters and Heirs; and that House was a Branch of the House of Morton, Issued thence about K Ed 3d time as may be perceived amongst Your Fathers Evidences and by Ecclesfield Church Windows, where there is in effect a Pedigree of that House as followeth, viz Alexandr Rokeby fillius Domini Tho: Rokeby de Richmondshire, /27 et quondam vico Comitis Eboracensis; Gulielmus Filius et Hæres Alexandri; Johannes Filius et Gulielmi; Thomas Filius et Hæres Johannis qui habuit duas Filias unam Nuptum Henrico Wombwell, Patri Nicholas Wombwell, Patris Thomæ Wombwell de Sincliff, Alteram nuptam Hugoni Searlaby de Searlabie et Harthill. In wch House in the Reign of K Henry 8th a good & Honest race of Brothers, lived in good places and Estimation. That is Sr Wm Rokeby Clerk Ld Archbishop of Dublin in Ireland, of whom ye Shall See Tombs at Dublin in Ireland; at Hallifax and Sandall in England. Sr Richard Rokeby Kt Controler to Cardinal Wolsey, The fourth Brother. The which Sr Rich lieth buried in the Savoy Church in the Strand, where you may See his Monument. He gave £200 towards the Building St Mary's Church in Beverley, where the Memorial is Engraven about a Wainscot near the Quire. He died without Issue, and Gave his Lands to Crake.

Tho Rokeby Esq the Eldest of those Brothers had issue only two Daughters, the one Married to Wombwell of Sinocliff, and the other to Searlabie of Searlabie, & Harthill, and Ralph Rokeby Esq Apprentice of the Laws; the Third of those Brothers of whom I find no mention, Save that he married Ann Holme, the Daug and Heir of John Holme, the Son of Robert Holme of Paul Holme ; and by her had Issue, Mary his Sole Daughter and Heire, married to William Rokeby, your Father. I Speak now to you Thomas, /²⁸ William, Ralph and Robert ; you must greatly grieve your Friends, and Shame your Selves, if you do not prove Worthies, that came on So good a Belley. I should do your Mother too great Wrong if I should not Testifie the Truth for Her, that She was a very Vertuous, Matron-Like young Woman ; a Loveing Wife to your Father, and a Hearty true Friend to his Friends whereoff myself felt assured Arguments ; that I could not but with many Tears bewayle her Untimely Death, as a Great Loss to your Father, your Selves and us all : and I know not how due regard of my Dear Dead Sister wrung out of me in a meer friendly vanitie, these Rhimes in her Remembrance,

I wonder pray from hence thou hop'st for Mary Rokeby
Mild and Good Lieth here Intombed ; a wife of vertues rare.
Whilear who Serv'd the Lord, her Husband dearly Lov'd,
Her Neigbours Cheared and Almes freely Show'd ;
    To Poors relief, her Loyall Loved Spouse
    Her Children, Poor, and friends of all her house
    Feels hurt & grief at this their grievous Cross,
    And Loud laments, their too too timely Loss.
    And you good wives which march in Honours trade
    (As She did erst) may deep fetched Sorrow brade ;
    But God hath her, yet ye do want her here,
    Whose Life in vertue Shin'd as Christall Clear ;
    And he that here hath brought her course to rest,
    And call'd her Soul above must aye be blest. Amen.
Viresit Funere.

And to you Thomas She assured a good £100 Land by'th year in Sandall and Thorngombald, and Left her self /²⁹ but an Estate for Life, Qualified by use to make Leases for 21 years ; and She also Enriched your Fathers House with the Mannors of Otringham and Kirton, Lands in Kingston upon Hull, Millton, Appleby, and Saxley.

Henry Rokeby the younger Son of John had Issue Cathrine Rokeby, one of his Co-Heirs, Married first to William Hawley, by whom she had Issue, Mary Their Daughter and Heir ; married to Sʳ John Stanhope, Son to Ed Stanhope Esq one of her majᵗⁱᵉ Councell in the North. And Isabell Rokeby his Second Daughter Married George Rokeby, Father to you My Younger Nephew Ralph Rokeby. Of your goodmen of Sandall I know nothing but by Fame of Former times delivered unto me by Men of more years then my Self, of whom I have heard that the Bishop was a Man of Great Hospitality, and thereby had the Vickaaridge of Hallifax, the whole parrish at his Beck and Command ; and that they were all honest and upright Men, and Dyed well beloved of Such as knew them ; and I may well ghess the Same by the places they Supply'd in ye Common Wealth ; Howbeit I must not forget that the Arch bishop built the Chappel in the North-East End of the

Church of Sandall, and left 100£ to his Executor   [sic]
Rickald to have had the Like builded on the other Side wherein the
s^d Rickald frustrated his Last Will and good Meaning, who Lived
then at Morton ; I believe that in K. Hen. 8^ths Reign, lived there
my Grandfather /^80 Ralph Rokeby, who by Margret Danby his Wife,
the Eldest of the 3 Coheirs of Danby of Yaffarth, and also Cozins
& Co-heirs with others of Sr Richard Conyers, K^t had Issue,
Thomas Rokeby, his Eldest Son ; John Rokeby his Second Son ;
Richard Rokeby his Third Son, & Ralph Rokeby, Serjeant at
Law, his Youngest Son and my good Father ; a Race of Right
good Brothers in my Opinion.

In the End of K. Hen. 8th his Raign, K Ed. 6 and Queen Mary ;
Lived then at Morton Thomas Rokeby Esqr Eldest to, and owner
of Morton ; a plaine man as might be, whose words came always
from his Heart, without faining, a Trusty Friend ; a froward Gent.
in the Field, and a Great House-Keeper ; whereby he rayned So
in the Good-will of his Country men, that his Son & Heir
Christopher Rokeby being assaulted at Quarterly Race by
Christopher Nevill, brother to the mighty Earl of Westmorland ;
whom the Earl had Sent thither with an Hundred men to kill him,
was both Defended & Guarded from the Violence of his Adver-
saries, and was able So to have rebounded the blows given him by
them, that they Should have Spilt the best blood in their Bodys,
if his part had been willing ; for then not a Gentleman in the field
but they Cryed, A Rokeby, a Rokeby ; But the Good old Thomas
/^81 being in Commission for the peace, Commanded and Intreated
peace (as he Said) yet it grieves me to Se him bleed that bleeds,
Yet keep the peace ; and therefore his King highly Loved him,
that could So well get the Love of his Country. He was at all
the Services against Scotland in his Time, a leader of Men, and left
to his Son and Heir Christopher Rokeby all the Appurtenances to
a Captain, as Guide of a Coat of Armes for Horsemen, now in the
House of Hotham (Bandioca Vecchia honordi Capitano,) Ensign of
Coulors for a Foot band, for a Tenth warr, Carrying. Drum all on
the top of Morton Hall, and of one Side thereoff Furniture for
many men, beside the Stow of the Square Tower ; He had Issue
by   [sic] Constable, a daughter of Everingham, Christopher his Eldest Son ; Ralph his Second Son ; Thomas his third
Son and Anthony his Youngest Son ; and   [sic] Daughter
married to Wickliff of Wickliff   [sic] Gower of Stansby,
          [sic] Jo. Dodsworth of Thornton, and Lancaster of
Stokebred ; Christopher the Eldest Son of the Said Thomas
Rokeby by   [sic] Lassells of Brackenbrough, had Issue
John his Eldest Son, and Roger, Dead without Issue, and
[sic] Daughters. John now living & our Chief owner of Morton,
hath Issue by   [sic] Twenge Thomas Rokeby now Liveing, hath Issue Ralph Rokeby my God Son, whom I pray God to
bless, and us all /^82 The Second of these Brethren Jo : Rokeby was

a Worthy Priest, and a D^r of Civill and Cannon Laws, of So
Exellent and profound Skill and Learning, that the parts beyond
the Seas; Arches at London; and the Court of Exchequer at
York, do yet resound of his great praise in that knowledge; Yea
it was Said of him for Laws as it was of Plato for Philosophy, (ipse
dixit) in the Course of 32 years that he Supplyed the Judicial place
at York, he never had Sentence admitted by Appeal but once;
and that was given by a Rash Chaplain of his, named Sr Anthony
Jonston, in his masters absence. He was also in his Childhood
Inclined to Chastyty, Shamefac'dness and Contempt of Riches,
Liberality, Integrity, and Hospitality: I could bring in Evident
proofs of them all, but I will recite but one or two, and leave you
for the rest to the Report of others Your friends; For Contempt
of Honour and riches he had, as I have heard say, Confirmed K.
Hen. 8th his Divorce from his Brother, Prince Arthurs wife being
of his Councell in that cause, and So confounded by the Common
Laws; The Popes absolute power arrogated to himself to dispence
with the Eternal Law of God, which prohibiteth the Brother to take
the Brothers Wife as Incest; For which the King, as I've heard say,
offer'd him the Bishopprick of London, but he refused, and chose
rather a Competent Liveing in the Church of York, with this word;
Nay, I pray /^{44} Your Grace, give Me rather Some poor Liveing in
any Country, far from Your Grace; And now whether his Desire
were moderate or no, I leave it to you and all good mens Considera-
tions. Assuredly in my Opinion he took a very wise resolution, for
I think him well happy who is well hidden. Of his Liberallity and
Hospitallity, all his Friends and many Strangers often tasted; Some
had of 100£, and more Sums, (as his nephews,) Christopher and
Anthony, my Self also: I do with bounden knowledge own to have
received of him, one time to Supply my Necessitys Ten pounds;
So did my Brother George Rokeby other Ten pounds to take his
Lease at Melton; So did my Sister Grace 20£ at her marriage,
with George Mackenworth Esqr. So did also a great Sort of poor
people at York, and elsewhere. And although his Table was open
to All, yet when any of his Friends had Suits before him, they were
barred to dine or Sup with him. If any Letters were Sent unto
him of any matter depending Judiciously before him, they were
openly read in the Face of the Court. K. Hen. 8th once Command-
ing him to give Sentence in a Cause of Matrimony, betwixt S^r
Anthony Lee and one of the Kings Favourites, he entreth it thus;
it is K^s pleasure, but against the Law. He was of the Councell
Establish't to assist the Lord president of the North; and in his
Latter /^{44} days was Sent into Scotland, with Sr Thomas Gargreaves
and others to reform the Laws of the Marches. Finally he Lived
a great Learned man, a good Councellor to his Prince, and Dyed
in Honourable gray Haires, a good Christian. Nostris jampridem
gloria Nominis; As I pray God we may all do. He lieth Buried
in York Minster, where hangeth a Table of Verses in his praise;

among which this one Sapphick pleasing me best I carried it away
in Memory

> Hic jacet tectus fragilis Sepulchro
> Ille Rokebeus pius atque justus
> Quem locat Summi Super astra clara
> Rector Olympi

I will not Stand to apply his good Life by every particular in our
Instruction, but desire you to make every Action of his Life, your
Direction, as the Musician Ismenias bad his schollers, when he
Shewed them Excellent plays on the Flute : So I bid you do as
he did.

Richard Rokeby, third Son of Ralph Rokeby, your great Grand-
father, a Servant and Soldier to the Lord Scroop of Bolton, whose
Standard he bare at Floddan Field, had Issue by Ellerker his
wife, a Daughter of Risbie, Thomas Rokeby who lived a Lusty
Servitor and an able leader of Men, who being one of the
Lieitenants to captain Ralph Ellerker his Cosin, appointed to
Serve on the Borders in the Middle Marches, for the Strength
thereoff against the Scots, by too much toyling himself in /ᵃᵇ the
Service, especially before the Muster Master at the Casting the
Bands, Melted his Grease within him, and came to my House at
York, and there Dyed without Issue ; an honest and a Brave
Soldier ; God Send the good Queen of England many Such at
her needs.

The fourth of these Brothers was Ralph Rokeby, Serjant at the
Common Laws ; Your Grandfather by the Father. I will not Say
more of him because he was my Father but that in the Skill of
his Science and other Good things, he was the Dᵐ Brother German
as well as by blood. He refused to be Lord Chief Justice of
England ; when Justice Morgan fell mad, he got a patent for his
discharge of the Attendance of the Common Law, and Served as
one of the Councell in the North. It hath done me good to hear
the old benchers of Lincolns Inn, Speak well of him Especially
S W Cordwell, Mʳ of the Rolls, who would often acknowledge
he had been in Effect Informed by him of the Laws of England ;
of whom one bound to him in Duty made the following English
verse

> Then Skill of Law he gained by Studious paines
> And it Employ'd to Prince and Countries well ;
> Who recompenc'd him here with Worldly gaines
> Alive and Dead his praises due forthtell :
> That he did Virtue Vance and Vice down Quell
> That the evills foe he was, the good mans friend,
> And pray god Send moe men of this mans Mind.

And he Dyed I thank God, in the Great good Love of his Country,
and Lyeth buried in Wakefield Church in Yorkshire : and Yet I
may not So Injuriously defraud my Father of his due praise as to
omitt his /ᵃᵇ Service against Sʳ Tho: Wyat, the Rebell of Kent,

against K Phillip: Queen Mary and the Spaniards being nois'd
to be comeing towards London; Your Grandfather went to
Westminster in his Serjeants Robes to plead; and under them a
Good Coat of Steel; and hearing at Charing Cross, the near
approach of the Rebells, he hastned him to the Queens Court at
Whitehall, Strung and fetled an Archer of the Guards Liverie
Bow, that Stood there Unstrung; threw down his Serjeants Robes
for that time, and went to the Gate house to Serve there wth a Bow
and a Sheaf of Arrows, and there tarried till the Enemy Yielded.
Old Nicholson of Pauls Chain told me my Father comitted a
Bagg of Money to keep, and that Alexander Metham his Clark
went with him, but Wm Bull hid him under my Fathers Bed in
Serjeants Inn, and there Lay till his Master Returned; and thus
in time of Need he was ready to fight against Rebells, to primer
on whom he had Jurisdiction in the Time of Peace in the Service
of Northampton, Warwick, Coventry, Leicester, Derby, Notting-
ham, Lincoln and Rutland, to adjudg of their Lives, Lands and
Goods; for their he was Justice of Assisses and Goal Delivery.
He by Dorothy Danby Daughter of Thomas Danby, and the son
of S^r   [sic] Danby and Grace Markham; had Issue four
Sons, Wm Rokeby Eldest Son, owner of Skyers Hall. Ralph
Rokeby the Writer hereoff, George Rokeby the Third Son, and
John Rokeby the Youngest; and 5 Daughters; Grace married to
George Mackenworth of Empringham /^87 in Rutlandshire, Esqr.
Dead without Issue; Frances Married to John Lathom, Minister,
by whom She hath Issue William Lathom, and   [sic]
Daughters. 3 Jane, married to Robert Byard, Gent, by whom
She hath Sons and Daughters. 4 Mary, married to William
Pulston Gent and Margery married to William Headly Gent.
[sic] Yeoman, by whom She hath had Issue Mary Headley. W^m
Rokeby of Skyers, Son of Ralph Rokeby, Serjeant of Lawe, an
Honest Lived man, a fearer of God, and a good Justice of Peace
in his Country, by Mary the Daughter and Heir of John Rokeby
of Kirk Sandal, his first Wife hath Issue Thomas, William, Ralph
my God Son and Robert his Youngest Son; and one Daughter
named Dorothy, to whom I pray God to Send a Good Husband &
to Encourage her that way, I may Safely and Truely Say, She
hath all the Likelihood to prove an Honest and a Thriving Hus-
wife. And you Tho. W^m and Ralph Rokeby, who all of you have
Served Her Majesty in the field before you were Nineteen Years
old; and You Thomas and William who have Served two French
kings both by Sea and Land, and Marched Continually both
Winter & Summer a Year together, and have been at the Winning
many Towns, that is, the Suburbs of Paris, Escarps, Jenvito,
Castran, Dux, Quindosm, Allencon, Mons, and Falaise, under the
General Charge of the Two peers of this Land, the Earl of Essex,
and that Noble Baron, the Lord Willoughby, and under the
Particular Leading, first of Captain Grevan, of Diep before the L^d

Willoughbies Arrivall /²⁸ in France; which brave and noble
Conductors only present and first Arrived in France; Raised the
Leaguers Siege of the King of Diep, when they were both in the
Camps within Musket Shot, one of the other, and under the
Conduct of Captain Chrismas, after you Wᵐ under the Conduct
of Captain Nicolas Basceruito; and Lastly under the Brave
Collonel Sʳ Roger Williams: at many other Services very my
good Wᵐ I will not wrong thee So far as far as to forget thee
carrying the Coll. Colours in the breach at the Takeing of Dreux
Castle this last Summer: and all this before a Hayre bud out of
their Chin. And my good Cosins I thank you both for your
Volley of Shot at the Funerall Convoy of my Learned Chamber-
fellow at Lincolns Inn Mʳ John Stubbs at in [sic] the Seas Sand
towards England, near Hav're-du-grace; for I commend to your
memories that in my Time Lincolns Inn Saw with two Eyes,
Wᵐ Lambert and John Stubbs; men of rare Learning and
Languages; of Civill piety to God, and Admirable vertues
among Men: Gods holy Name be prais'd who hath hitherto
preserved you among the Bullets, and will no Doubt, perfect you
Still in good Doing & Makeing pursuit after the Purchase of
Honour in the field, as I trust you will, and pray God you may
do.

Ralph Rokeby 2ⁿᵈ Son of Ralph Rokeby, Serjeant at Law by
his first Wife Douglas, Daughter of Wᵐ Ferne of Doncaster Esqr;
had no Issue. She lived with him but a Year and about a
Fortnight; an Honest young woman, and a Lowly and Lovely
Wife; of whose Death, to comfort her Husband, Wᵐ Cambden
writ these verses /²⁹

In Obitū optimæ, et Castissimæ Mulieris
Douglasiæ Rokebei Suavissimæ Uxoris,
Radulphi Rokebye Epitaphium
Duglasiam junxit Rokebœo jure jugalis
 Una Fides, Unum fœdus, et unus Amor
Utrique æqualis urebant Pectora Flamma
 Ille bonus, melior Sed tamen illa Fuit
Illa Fidem Christo defixit, Fida Marito
 Unica Spes Matris, deliciæq. Patris
Illa pudica, Decens, Humilis, Pia, Provida, mitis
 Omnibus et animi, Conspicienda Bonis
Vidit, et invidit, Mors improba jussit ut illa
 Cederet et Vita, parvit illa Libens
Parvit et tenebra, æterno Lumine mutans
 Jam Christo vivit perfruiturque Deo.

And then also Inter Suspira et Lachrymas, These Comforts burst
forth from the Same Learned Mʳ Cambden;

Flore velim Sed flore vetat mens obruta Luctu
 Introrsus Lachrymas Imbibit ipsæ Dolor
Utque Dolor major quam fletus fundere possit
 Egerit invito flentia verba tamen
Que major potiorq. mei pars optima conjux

Mortua divisit, viscera morte mihi
Illa mihi charo fuerat perchara marito
Illa mihi columen, presidiumque fuit
Illa quies Thalami, postrema et Prima Voluptas
Illa mihi consors, et mihi Dulce decus
Illa Patri Matrique Sua charissima proles
Sed tamen Æterno charior illa patri
Hanc mihi preripuit fatum fœdusque jugale,
/⁴⁰ Vix junctam rupit Mors properata nimis,
Linquerit ut citius vesani Somnia Mundi
Certius et Superas possit audire domes ;
Chare vale conjux, quid flentia verbula prosunt
Quæ tua Mors nobis est tibi vita Deo
Non amissa Mihi tamen es præmissa Sed illus
Quo te cum fati incerit [sic] jusserit ordo, Sequar
Douglasia interea Rokebœi pectore clausa,
Rokebœo Memori mente Superstes erit.

To these may be added Rob⁺ Cais friendly remembrances : viz.

Heu quanta est avido, permissa Licentia fato
Nill Pietatis amor, nil pulchra gratia formæ
Cuncta Simul Potuere, nihill nam viva fuisset
Femina, tantarum Laudum Stipata caterva
Sed jam pallentes (indigne) mersa Sub umbras
Occidit sed [sic] et moriens animam, vitamque reliquit
Fallar ego, Cecidisse nequit, Concendit aulam
Ætheris, et vivens animam, Vitamque resumpsit.

He after Married Joan, Daughter of John Portington of Portington Esq⁺ and Ann Laughton, Daughter of John Laughton, of
Laughton in Lincolnshire, Esq⁺ of whose Marriage their Loving
friend Thomas Leach writ the following Verses : viz.

Adsis Musa precor, non omnia possumus omnes,
Huc ades, et vati fer opem mihi diva recenti :
En mihi per Somnum, xaj y το ουας εη Διι erj [1]
Jupiter a Summo descendens lætus olympo
Conubio Equalis conjungere Visus Amantes
Incipe fœlices tædas Celebrare Thalia
/⁴¹ Diique Deæque omnes Hymenæum quique Soluti,
Huc omnes fecere auditum Sua dona ferentes
Mercurius pura donat, virtute maritum,
Dulcis et Uxori formam Venus addit amœnam
Munere nec tali Pallas Divina Carebat
Incipe Fœlices tædas celebrare Thalia
Exornata micat regali Splendida gaza
Tota Domus Cereris his Copia, Copia Bacchi
Ast ego Surrexi visus non immemor hujus
Fama volens tandem nostras pervenit ad Aures
Que Somnus Docuit post Exitus ingens
Incipe felices tædas celebrare Thalia
Hanc Laudate Diem, qua non jucundior ulla est
Nobis o juvenes, generoso Sanguine natus
Uxorem dignam, Rokebeus duxit, et aptam
Illis pulchra datur, puerisque beata creandis Uxor,
Incipe felices tædas Celebrare Thalia
O Læta Lætus Vivat, cum conjuge conjux

---

[1] The transcriber evidently failed to decipher the latter part of this line.   Probably he did
not know Greek sufficiently to copy the letters correctly.   I have done my best to reproduce
his attempt.—ED.

Illis mella Fluant, ferat et rubus asper amomum
Omnia Succedant ut ima Fœliciter illis
Condida Quos pietas, puroque in pectore fixus
Junxit amor bonus, et felici cum alite Virtus
Incipe Fœlices tædas Celebrare Thalia
Ulmos vitis amat conjux amat alma maritum
Ut rosa Flos florum, decus ac Sit dulce maritus
Uxores veres Sit amor, conjunctus Honore
Plaudite dum Licet, Est Hymenei nobile nomen
Ludite nam Servit pueris alma Venus creandis
Incipe Fœlices tædas Celebrare Thalia
O certe volo, O volo Rokebeus parvulus olim
Incipiat plaudo risu cognoscere partrem
Equet virtutem propria virtute paternam
Exuperat proavos fæmæque, et Laudis Honore
/⁴³ Sit decus eximium, et generosa gloria gentis
I Mæcanatis nostri te confer ad ædes
Hoc carmen Læto cantato voce Thalia.

By which his now good Wife he had Issue Rose Rokeby his Eldest Daughter, dead without Issue And now hath Issue Ann Rokeby, to whom god grant Grace to live in his Faith and Dye in his fear. Ann was Married to Sʳ John Hotham of Skerbrough. George Rokeby 3ᵈ Son of Ralph Rokeby, Serjeant at Law; had by his first Wife Joan; (The Second Daughter, and one of the Coheirs of Henry Rokeby of Kirk Sandall) had Issue Rich Rokeby his Eldest Son, dead without Issue. And you my younger Nephew Ralph Rokeby, Dorothy, Cathrine, Bridget; and by his Second Wife, Elizabeth Ferne, the Widdow of Anthony Rothwood, (late deceased) Fayles Rokeby, all whom I pray God to bless, Amen.

John the Youngest Son of Ralph Rokeby, Serjeant at Law, by Margery the Daughter of Thomas Westly of Ranfield, Gent, hath Issue Thomas, The Image of a Good Uncle.

And the Said four Brethren, Sons of Your Great grandfather had also a Right Worthy Matron to their Sister, called Phillips, Married to John Scroop, Esqʳ Brother to the afternamed Lord Scroop of Bolton, By whom She had Issue, the House of Scroop now planted in Richmondshire Hampshire and Buckingham-shire, /⁴³ and 3 Daughters, one Married to Christopher Wyvill Esqʳ Another to Thornesby Esqʳ and a Third to Thomas Moore Esq and thus much of this Brotherhood.

There resteth Somewhat now for me to Speak of the Line of Thomas Rokeby, the Eldest of these Brothers; He had Issue by Jane Daughter of Robert Constable of Cliff, Serj at Law; Christopher Rokeby, who was one of the Defenders of Haddington unto Sʳ James Willford, a Captain of Musceleborroug-Field; and at Leith, and Captain of Norram Castle, at Norram Chase; Lost by Some whom I name not, for the reverence I bear unto the House. He is a Deserving man, and hath yearly paid by Her Maj out of the Exchequer, 100 pounds for Some Servis done in Scotand; what it was I know not, but it did greatly Endanger his Life; and Turner his man was once in Scotland turned over the Gallows before his pardon came ; but Since that time he was the Provost Marshall of the Field, and Captain of 300 men against the rebells in the North, in the Eleventh year of Her Maj Reign. The Same Thomas had Issue Ralph Rokeby who Dyed at St Cathrines in London, and was never married. His Second Son who was Apprentice at the Law, and is yet A Counsellour ; assistant to the Lord President of the North. He also before that Supply'd the Roome of Her Matie Justice of   [sic] in Ireland under Sr Edward Fitton, Kt. L$^{d.}$ President thereoff, to his great Charges, and also to his good Credit. /^{44} My acquaintance, Henry Catline who Served with him in the Field there, told me that at every allarm, the Velvet Jack was first put on, and the Soldiers drunk Sack of his Charges. He was after named Lord Chancellor of Ireland, but he made Friends to Shun it. And God bless long our good and Gracious Queen of England, Queen Elizabeth, who hath Since given him for Recompence of good Service, Mastership of St Katharines ; and made him one of the Masters of Request to her Maj^{ty} and truly he hath much good in him, God be thanked for him, and Bless him, Amen. Nostræ nunc decus Familiæ, That old Thomas had also Issue, Thomas Rokeby his 3^d Son whom I mention with Reverence, for that he continually beareth about him an Air and Ensign of Valour, And Honourable Service done to his Country for being at Norram Chase, Lieutenant to his Brother Christopher Rokeby, he had a speare broken in his Face ; after he in the Chase Dismounted him self, to mount his Captain, who had his Horse Slain under him, where exposeing himself to all Dangers for his Brothers deliverance, he was taken Prisoner when others fled.

He by Catharine Leighe, his Wife, Sister to Urian Leigh of Adlington in Cheshire ; had Issue William Rokeby his eldest Son, now owner of Hotham ; and Ralph Rokeby his Second Son, and 2 Daughters Elizabeth and Susan ; whom god grant them Grace to follow their forefathers Steps in Virtue

/^{45} William Rokeby of Hotham Married the daughter of William Rokeby Esq of Skyers, and hath Issue by her, William, Alexander, Thomas and Phillip ; and one Daughter married to Christopher Ledyard of Anlabie Esq.

William Rokeby the Eldest Son of William of Hotham (a worthy, kind Gentleman, and Loveing to his Kindred) married the Daughter of Sr Wm Hickman of Gainsborough K^t by whom he hath Issue his Eldest Son William ; 2 Alexander, Willoughby, Francis, Charles and 2 Daughters.

Alexand^r the Second Son of old W^m of Hotham was Married to Susanna the Daughter of Gervase Bossevill Esqr of Warmsworth ; by whom he hath Issue William and Alexander 2 Sweet babes, whom I pray God to Bless with his Choicest Blessings.

[Half a page blank.]

/[46] Now it resteth for Conclusion, that I commend to your memory Some places where you may find Some monuments and places where are Antiquities of y[r] Ancestors; wherein I will not observe the Dignities of the places, but the Suit of Time; The place of greatest Antiquity where our Ancestors was Buried was Egleston Abbey, near the Toun of Rokeby; yea So near that it Devoured up a good Share thereoff in the Demeans. A pretence of Holyness haveing Drawn our Ancesters by the Zeal of Devotion, where with they were with the Blindness of those times carried away, to repute it a great Step towards Heaven, to have their Burials in those places, or amongst those parties, or at least in those habits, whose unhallowed Shows and outward Shells of Piety, appearing to the Eternal Eye that Searcheth both Hearts & Reins, and pierceth to the   Dividing the Marrow & bone; yea the Soul and Body; to be a Meer Pageant of Hypocrisy, and their Intollerable pride, unsatiable Covetuousness, the foul Dissolution of their Lewd Lives, and most abominable Idollatries; Ascending to the Almighty Judg of Heaven and Earths high Justice Seat, and there Crying against them Vengeance for Sin. Almighty God in his most Just & high Displeasure against Rebellious Sinners, hath by the Breath of his Nostrils thrown them and their Cells into utter Ruin, & Desolation So that I am Seges et Herba Est ubi /[47] fuerant Templa fratram, colunt q, nunc monumenta Patrum. And the Ancesters of the House of Bowes and Rokeby Lye without Doors, in the Demaynes of Egglestone Abby; where yet their Grave Stones appear old and Weather beaten. Next to that is the Nursery of Arms that I could never See in England; Selby Church in Yorkshire; Converted from a Conventicle to a Parrochial Church; where on the Right Side of the Quire is our Coat Arms in the first place in the Dexter Point of that Window; and next to that is Lowthers Coat of Lowther in Westmoreland, our Kinsman, Married I think to S[r] Thomas Rokebys Daughter. Then the new Cathedral Church at Durham, where our Armes were Set up at the Service of Durham field, (as I Suppose) against the Scots. Wath Church Standing near Dearn harboureth our Coal, which Seemeth very Antiently to be possessed of the Same. Ecclesfield Church in Yorkshire, hath also our Armes in the Windows and Monuments Derived from about Rich[d] 2[ds] Time, and Henry 4th. The Cathedral of Dublin in Ireland, Kirk Sandal, Hallifax Church as M[r] Rob[t] Waterhouse, his Father told me, when I was his Steward of Hallifax Court, and may also appear by the Copy of his Testimony remaining in the Hands of William Rokeby of Skyers.

S[t] Mary's Church at Beverly hath carved about a great Stall in the body of the Church, next to the Quire this record of S[r] Richard Rokeby /[48] and Jane his Wife as followeth: viz. Lord have mercy of all the Souls of Men, Women and Children, whose bodys were Slain at the falling of this Church, which were 55.

d

The fall was the 29th of April 1526. And for the Souls of them that have been good Benefactors & Helpers of this Church up again; and for all Christian Souls which God would have Prayed for; and for the Souls of Sr Richard Rokeby Knight and Dame Jane his Wife, who gave 200£ toward the Rebuilding this Church; and for the Souls of William Hall Cooper and his Wife. This caution I thought good to give the reader, that this Prayer must be understood of Thanksgiving to God for the Deads good Deeds and Examples; otherwise it is false Doctrine, and against Scripture which Teacheth the particular Judgment of the Soul to be at Departure of the Soul and Body. As touching the foremention'd History I have heard that a Bear baiting and a Mass being both at once, there was near 1000 people at 2 Bear baitings; and but only 55 at Mass, who were all Slain. And ever Since they Say there, It is better to be at the Baiting of a Bear then at the Saying of a Mass. The Same man being also a Benefactor to the House of Savoy in the Strand, hath left a fair Monument of his Burial there. On Greta Bridge are the Coat Armes of Bowes and Rokeby in Stone. In our Cousin Lassells House at Mawburn in the Hall Windows is our Coat Armes. In our Cousin Lowthers House at Penrith, is the match of Sr Hugh Lowther (a Brave Knight) with our Ancestor /⁴⁹ Sr Thomas Rokebys Daughter, in a Tapistry Covering. And also in our late Cosin Thomas Wombwells of Syn o cliff Hall Windows at Syn o cliff Grange, is the Coat of Rokeby of Sandall. If they be not at Askew his house in Lincolnshire; I think they are at Lincolns Inn in the North East corner Chamber. Also I plac'd our Coat Armes with my very Loveing Chamber fellows Charles Chaulthorpes, John Tyndall and John Stubbs; where we seemed, there the Chamber for the most part was well furnished, and the Windows Richly beautified. And for good Mr Stubbs, I highly thank God for him, for the Correcting many unruly humours in me, and trayning me into the path to God, and his fear and Service; And now my good Cosins, that our good and gratious God hath given us these goodly Temporal Blessings here in Earth, to have our living and Descent from these our good and honest Ancestors, of whom I write with Joy, and Cannot but think of them with Comfort; it behooveth us to propound their Vertues before our Eyes, for patterns of the Actions of our Lives, that they may be Spurrs and Pricks to us, to carry our Selves, and addict us Especially to build up Gods Church, and to the Propagation of Gods Glory and his Gospell, in all true Loyalty and Dilligence to our King and Country of England in all Duty and Humility to our Superiours and Governours, In lowly Gentillity and friendly Courtesy with our Equals, in a Loveing neighbourhood with our Inferiors /⁵⁰ to be Gentle and Quiet at home in peace; to be brave and forward with the foremost in the field. No Lewd Brawlers, no Whore Mast^{rs}, No Ale Hunters; fie that ever a Gentle name should be

Impeached there with, or that we should ever enter an Ale House
or Tavern of Tinkers, Rogues, Whores and Thieves; And be so
far from Prideing our Selves in others Plumes, as always for
Morral Vertues and Good Services to our King and Country. To
think of my very good friend and fellow in Lincolns Inn, M^r
John Tindalls word of Arms, Propria quemq. And yet I tell you
he beareth the Coat Armes of the Crown of Bohemia, where (by
Felbrigs Daughter and Heir) he is Lineally Descended, And
that whensoever a proud Thought arisith in our Hearts, none of
those our Worthy fore fathers Vertues, Honours, or Services
appertain unto us. Nay, whensoever a proud thought Swelleth
our Hearts, we Should (but for Christianitys Sake) with a Dagger
Dig it out. A Gentle Heart Riseth a foot in the belly at a proud
mind, wheresoever it Encountereth it, and Abhoreth and Contem-
neth it as the Gate of Hell. No, our Behaviour must declare,
that we carry the Marks and Badges of our Blessed Lord and
Saviour Jesus Christ Crucified; and therefore in his Holy
Name and fear, must Humble our Selves before Almighty God;
and with Hearts and Hands thrown /⁶¹ up to Heaven Bless God,
who of his Great Goodness amongst many Gifts and Graces both
of this Life and that to come, hath given us out of one and our
own Family these Good Examples of Vertue and Vallour; and
must Sing with the Royall Psalmist, Non Nobis Domine, non
Nobis Sed Nomini tuo donius Gloriam. And we must always pray
to God after his Holy Will and Pleasure; to continue our Family
in a Posterity that may fear God, and follow Vertue Amen. And
I hope I may Wish (without offence) this Good Success to our tree
of Kindred

Cresces Diu Fælix arbos ; Semperque vireto
Frondibus ut nobis talia pomo feras

Amen Good Lord

1	Time	Sr Alexander Rokeby K^t Married	} {	Sr Humphry Listles his Daughter
2		Ralph his Son Married	} {	Thomas Lumley's Daughter
3		Thomas Rokeby K^t Married	} {	Thomas Hubborns Daughter
4		Ralph Rokeby K^t Married	} {	Sr Ralph Bigotts Daughter
5		Thomas Rokeby K^t Married	} {	Sr John de Nelsars Daughter, of Bener Hall in Holderness
6		Ralph Rokeby Esqr Married	} {	Sr Bryan Stapletons Daughter of Wighell

/ss 7	Time	Thomas Rokeby Kᵗ Married	} {	Sʳ Ralph Uries Daughter
8	Ed. 2	Ralph Rokeby Married	} {	The Daughter of Mansfield Heir of Morton
9	Ed. 3	Thomas Rokeby Kᵗ Married	} {	Strood Daughter & Heir
10	Hen. 4	Ralph Rokeby Kᵗ Married	} {	Sʳ James Strangways Daughter
11		Thomas Rokeby Esqʳ Married to	} {	Sʳ John Hothams Daughter
12	Hen. 7	Ralph Rokeby Esqʳ Married to From this man is Descended the House of Skyers and of the fourth Brother	} {	Danby of Yafforths Daughter & Heir
13	Hen. 8 Ed. 6 Mary	Thomas Rokeby Esqʳ Married to	} {	Robᵗ Constables Daughter of Cliff Serjeant Law
14		From the above named Thomas Rokeby is Descended the House of Hotham and of the 2 Brother		
		Christopher Rokeby Married to	} {	Lassells of Brackenburies Daughter
15		John Rokeby Married to	} {	The Daughter of Twenge
16		Thomas Rokeby Kᵗ Married to	} {	Sʳ Ralph Lawsons Daughter of Brough
17		Francis Rokeby his Son married to	} {	Flawcet of
18				
19				

Ex dono Thomæ Rokebye fratris
Georgij Rokebye, et Rectoris de
Warmsworth Rectoriæ Evoracensis
Live well, Die never:
Dye well, Live ever.

THO ROKEBY

This was Left a great while, and after-
-wards found and Renewed by the Same
Ralph Rokeby, Jan. 30ᵗʰ 1593

Finisht this Transcript May yᵉ 20ᵗʰ 1712
By W. Jackson
(End of Manuscript.)

APPENDIX I.

ADDITIONAL ROKEBY PEDIGREE.

THOMAS ROKEBY of Mortham was eldest son of Francis Rokeby and his wife Susanna, daughter of James Fawcett (not Flawcet, as in p. 32), citizen of London; baptized at Rokeby 1640; buried in London 1703; married, 1661, Margaret, daughter of John Wycliffe, Esq. of Gates, Co. York; she died 1703. He had issue:—1. Christopher, who succeeded; 2. Thomas, b. 1666, d. 1667; 3. Francis, b. 1669; 4. Ralph, b. 1670, alive 1722; 5. William, b. 1672; 6. Joseph, b. 1674, married Catherine Bowes, and had issue: (a) Thomas, b. 1720; (b) Catherine, b. 1718; 7. Mary, b. 1662; 8. Susanna, b. and d. 1664; 9. Mildred, b. 1678, alive 1714; 10. Margaret, b. 1667, d. 1668; 11. Elizabeth, b. 1676, married Peter Save, alive 1714.

Christopher, eldest son, b. 1664, mar. at Rokeby, 1697, Anne Sanderson, who died 1737. He had issue:—1. Peter, yeoman, b. 1698, d. 1761; 2. Christopher, b. 1707, d. 1772—it is not known if these left issue; 3. William, of whom below; 4. Elizabeth, b. 1702; 5. Anne, b. 1704.

William, 3d son, b. 1699, mar. Jane ——, who died 1766; he died 1783, leaving issue:—1. William, who succeeded; 2. Joseph, b. 1737, d. 1771; 3. Francis, b. 1743, d. 1755; 4. Anne, b. 1731, mar. 1753, Francis Appleby of Barningham.

William, eldest son, joiner, b. 1734, mar., 1763, Margaret, daughter of John and Elizabeth Mewburn (and died 1826, aet. 86, having married, 2d, —— Danby, a miner). William Rokeby was drowned at Clapgate Beck 1771, leaving issue:—1. William, who follows; 2. Elizabeth, b. 1764, mar. Peter Seneschall of Highgate, and died s.p. 1819; 3. Jane, b. 1768, d. 1846.

William, eldest son, a saddler in London, b. 1771, d. June 16, 1823, having married at St. Andrew's, Holborn, Ann, eldest daughter of Richard and Ann Jones of Shenley, Co. Herts; she died April 1850, aet. 49. Issue:—1. William, b. 31 July 1814, a saddler, Gray's Inn Lane, London, d. 1850, having mar., about 1846-7, Hannah, 4th daughter of Richard Robinson of Yorkshire; he had issue: (a) Hannah, b. 1849, d. 1870; (b) William, b. 1850, d. 1850; 2. Ann, b. 16 March 1802, d. April 1842; 3. Margaret, b. 3 Aug. 1803, d. ——; 4. Elizabeth, b. 6 Oct. 1805, mar. George Roberts, and had issue 2 sons and 4 daughters; 5. Jane, b. 20 March 1808, d. 1861; 6. Sarah, b. 28 May 1810, mar., 1837, John Davies, and has issue 4 sons and 5 daughters; 7. Mary, b. 3 Sept. 1812, d. 1868; 8. Ralph, who follows; 9. Emma, b. 3 March 1820, mar., 1847, Enos Purcell, d. s.p. 1857.

Ralph, 2d son, b. 3 Oct. 1816, in H.M.C.S., In. Rev., mar., 1st, at Liverpool, 21 Feb. 1843, Frances, eld. daughter of James and Mary Dodge; she died 1860; he married, 2dly, Emily, 3d daughter of William Reach of Gretton Wood Lodge, Rockingham Forest, Co. Northam. He has issue by first wife only: 1. William, who follows; 2. Mary, d. 1864; 3. Ann; 4. Isabella, d. 1847; 5. Thomas, b. 31 March 1849, mar. at Ware, 1878, Elizabeth, daughter of William S. Welsman, and has issue: (a) Ethel, (b) Mary; 5. Ralph, b. 1 July 1850, mar., 1885, Emma Childs; 6. James, b. and d. 1851; 7. Charles, b. and d. 1852; 8. Isabella, b. and d. 1856.

William, H.M.C.S., b. 23 Jan. 1847, mar., Sep. 16, 1872, Helena, daughter of Joseph Stringer of Maidstone, and has issue: 1. William Ralph, b. 13 Oct. 1873; 2. Frank, b. 2 Jan. 1875; 3. Philip, b. 6 March 1876; 4. Leonard, b. 24 April 1877 (dead); 5. Ralph, b. 24 April 1879; 6. Thomas, b. 1884; 7. Emily; 8. Gertrude.

The Pedigree of the Rev. H. Ralph Rokeby of Arthingworth, descended from Thomas Rokeby of Mortham, who married Robert Constable's daughter (p. 32), will be found in Burke's *Landed Gentry*, 5th edition, 1871, p. 1185.

APPENDIX II.

ROKEBY.—To complete the Pedigree of the Rokeby family the following works may be profitably consulted. I am indebted for most of the references to Dr. Marshall's most valuable *Genealogist's Guide* (2d edition). Surtees Society, xxxvi. 73, 167, 184, 372, xli. 40 ; *Gentleman's Magazine*, 1825, ii. 212 ; Burke's *Commoners*, iv. 666 ; *Landed Gentry*, 2, 3, 4, 5, 6 ; Foster's *Yorkshire Pedigrees;* Foster's *Visitations of Yorkshire,* 128, 199, 352, Harleian Society, viii. 426, xvi. 268 ; Thoresby's *Ducatus Leodiensis,* 255 ; *Archæologia Æliana,* 2d Series, v. 19 ; Hunter's *Deanery of Doncaster,* i. 203, ii. 102 ; Plantagenet Harrison's *History of Yorkshire,* i. 407, 410 ; *Yorkshire Archæological and Topographical Journal,* vi. 202 ; Burke's *Extinct Baronetcies* ; Scott's *Poetical Works* (Author's Edition, 1869), App. to ' Rokeby,' 364 ; *Transcript of the Registers of St. Mary Woolnoth and St. Mary Woolchurch, London,* 307, 308, 309, 345 ; Rudder's *Hist. of Gloucestershire* (Dymock Parish) ; Haine's *Man. of Brasses,* ii. 153, 227 ; Estcourt's *English Catholic Nonjurors,* 173 ; *Transcript of Registers of St. Dionis Backchurch,* Harl. Soc. ; *Cal. State Papers, Scot.,* i. 233, 236, 255 ; Whittaker's *Hist. of Richmond,* i. 157-183 ; Stow's *Survey of London* (ed. 1842), 145 ; *London Mar. Licences,* Harleian Society, vols. xxiii. xxiv. xxv. xxvi. ; Nicholas' *Testamenta Vetusta,* 723 ; Kimber's *Baronetage* (Hotham) ; *Retrospective Review,* 2d Series, vol. ii. (1828).

BOYLSTON.—Members of the Boylston Family are mentioned in the following works :—Burton's *Hist. of Bewdley* ; *Transcript of Registers of St. Mary Woolnoth and St. Mary Woolchurch* ; Beriah Botfield's *Stemmata Bottevilliana;* Visitation of Staffordshire, by H. S. Grazebrook ; *Visitation of Gloucestershire,* Harleian Society ; *Cal. State Papers, Dom. Ser.,* A.D. 1637, p. 149 ; Hotten's *List of Persons sent to America; Rep. of Commission on MSS. in Private Possession,* vi. 135 ; *Transcript of Registers, St. Anthony, London Wall; Transcripts of Registers of St. Dionis Backchurch, London ;* Harwood's *History of Lichfield.* A Pedigree of the Boylstons of New England has been printed in America, showing that President Adams was a descendant of Thomas Boylston, the father of Dr. Zabdiel Boylston.

HALLEN (VAN HALEN).—*An Account of the Hallen Family,* by A. W. Cornelius Hallen, has been privately printed. There is a copy in the Brit. Mus. Lib., and in the Guildhall Library.

APPENDIX III.

The table on the next page will show the Pedigree of the present owner of Mr. Boylston's copy of *Œconomia,* and how the MS. came into his possession. A copy of the *Œconomia* exists at the Leeds Library. Both the Rev. H. R. Rokeby, and R. Rookeby, Esq., possess a modern copy. Whittaker, in his *History of Richmond,* has printed most of the work, but does not say what MS. he made use of.

Letters in the possession of the Rev. H. R. Rokeby (dated 1825) show that the original MS. was in existence in the beginning of the century, and was written on two rolls of parchment, one three or four yards in length. Mr. Langham Rokeby used to say that Sir Walter Scott borrowed it when preparing the notes to ' Rokeby,' and that it was never returned. If this is the case it may still be possible to trace it. The Editor would be glad of any information. Whittaker refers to ' Mr. Scott's ' acquaintance with it.

ARMS.

Arms of ROKEBY (p. 8) : *arg.* a chevron, *sa.* between 3 rooks proper. *Crest,* a rook proper.
Arms of BOYLSTON (p. 3) : *sa.* six cross crosslets fitchée on a chief, *arg.* 3 bezants. *Crest,* a lion passant holding a cross fitchée *or.*
Note : on Mr. Richard Boylston's signet seal, penes J.C.H. the chief is *or,* 3 Torteaux.
Arms of VAN HALEN OF MALINES : quarterly 1, and 4 *gu.* a lion ramp. *or,* armed, langued, and crowned *as.* Mirabelle. 2 and 3 *as.* on a bend between 2 estoiles *or,* 3 roses *gu.* leaved *vert.* seeded *or,* van Halen. *Crest* a demi-lion as in the arms, between two wings *sa.*

PORTIONS OF THE PEDIGREES OF THE FAMILIES OF ROKEBY BOYLSTON, AND HALLEN.

(Owners of Transcript of *Œconomia Rokebiorum*.)

Rokeby.

GEORGE ROKEBY, 'citizen of London,' brother of Thomas R., Rector of Warmesworth (see p. 18), possessed a copy of *Œconomia Rokebiorum* (p. 32) which was transcribed in 1712 for his grandson, Richard Boylston. G. R. died 1656.

= GRACE UNDERWOOD, daughter of Robert Underwood, of the county of Hertford; died 1673.

Boylston.

HENRY BOYLSTON, 'Gentleman,' of the city of Lichfield, of the Boylstons of Staffordshire, a family of repute mentioned in various Visitations, but no Pedigree recorded, 2d cousin of Dr. Zabdiel Boylston (p. 3) of New England.

= RHODA ROKEBY (see pp. 18, 38), died 1704. Will at Lichfield. See Foster's sheet Pedigree of Rokeby.

Hallen.

CORNELIUS VAN HALEN, 'Esquire,' 7th in lineal descent from Sir Francis van Halen, K.G., who was honoured with a public funeral at Malines, 1375, and was grandson of John de Mirabelle dit van Halen, a Lombard, who in consequence of an alliance with the heiress of Halen assumed that name. Cornelius van Halen was born at Malines, 1581, and came to London 1610; he was alive in 1654, was in the Commission of the Peace for the county of Surrey, and a 'Pan-maker.'

= MARGARET ——, first wife, buried at St. Olaves, Southwark, 1625.

RICHARD BOYLSTON, = · · · · · 'Apothecary,' of Birmingham; died about 1750. R. B. had a son Rokeby, who died young. See Registers St. Martin's, Birmingham.

CORNELIUS HALLEN, 2d son, 'Pan-maker'; buried at Stourbridge, 1682.

= CONSTANCE ——, first wife; buried at Stourbridge, 1653.

WILLIAM HALLEN, eldest son, 'Pan-maker'; buried at Stourbridge, 1715.

= MARGARET ——

CORNELIUS HALLEN, 2d son, 'Pan-maker'; b. 1673, buried at Madeley, Salop, 1744. Great-great-grandfather to A. W. Cornelius Hallen.

JOHN HALLEN, 3d son, 'Pan-maker'; b. 1679, buried at Birmingham, 1763.

= ELIZABETH CLAY, b. 1690, d. 1750; an heiress (?), arms on old seal, penes J. C. H. arg. on a chevron between three trefoils sa. three plates.

DAVID HALLEN, 2d son, 'Pan-maker'; b. 1719, buried at Birmingham, 1789; unmarried.

JOHN CLAY HALLEN, eldest son, 'Attorney-at-Law'; b. 1714, buried at Birmingham, 1770.

= SARAH BOYLSTON, only surviving child; b. 1717, d. 1802.

JOHN BOYLSTON HALLEN, 'Gentleman'; b. 1752, d. 1797.

= CHARLOTTE TURNER; b. 1751, d. 1844.

JOHN TURNER HALLEN, 'Captain in the Army'; b. 1785, buried at London, 1877.

= ANN MARSHALL, d. 1870.

ROKEBY BOYLSTON HALLEN, 'Gentleman,' third, but only married son; b. 1838, d. 1870.

= HANNAH BRADSHAW.

JOHN CHARLES HALLEN; b. 1865. In whose possession Rich. Boylston's Transcript of George Rokeby's copy of the *Œconomia*, here printed, now is.

ANN ELIZABETH HALLEN.

VARIOUS READINGS

(From H. R. Rokeby's MSS. *except marked* (W.) *for Whittaker's.)*

' Tum felix domus est, et tum numerosa supellex
Quum pius est domus, et bene parta domus.'

ŒCONOMIA ROKEBEIORUM

Written by RALPH ROKEBY, ESQ[1]
ye Younger of Lincolns Inn.

In Nomine Patris, Filii, et Spiritus Sancti. Amen.

To my very good Nephews, Thomas, William, Ralph, Robert, and
Ralph Rokebys.

Page 5, line 4, ' viz. ob !' omitted. l. 5, for ' from Good to Evil' read ' ill to worse.'
l. 19, for ' be affrighted' read ' being.' l. 27, for ' prickle' read ' prick.' l. 24, all from ' for
to use,' etc., to ' pleasures,' l. 28, in a parenthesis. l. 30, ' and to be,' leave out ' and.' l. 32,
for ' courage' read ' carriage.' l. 34, for ' seasoning taketh' read ' season taketh the Taste,
thereof for the most part keepeth a long time the savour.' l. 47, for ' appeared' read
' appeareth.'
Page 6, line 5, for ' in Trinity' read ' of the Trinity.' l. 8, for ' no way' read ' no way
else.' l. 9, for ' everlasting Godhead' read ' everlasting justice in the flesh.' l. 11, for ' all
just, all perfect God and Man' read ' all perfect and all just, God and man.' l. 13, for
' inaccessibleness of God' read ' majesty inaccessible of God's wisdom.' l. 14, after ' satisfy'
insert a semicolon, and delete semicolon after ' man.' l. 15, after ' Jesus Christ' insert ' by
His Precious Death.' l. 16, for ' that day' read ' in that.' l. 17, for ' forth' read ' for ; ' for
' praised' read ' raised.' l. 18, for ' Bodies' read ' Bonds. l. 21, for ' left up' read ' lifted
Himself up ; ' for ' where' read ' whence.' l. 26, for ' in His Apostles' read ' by His Apostles.'
ll. 27 and 28, ' and Bequest' omitted ; for ' by His,' etc., read ' with His to shed.' l. 31, for
' It' read ' Him.' l. 33, for ' that the Holy Trinity hath done' read ' hath the Holy Trinity
done.' l. 38, for ' Lives' read ' Faith.' l. 39, ' but upon' read ' but if upon.' l. 40, after
' conference' read ' it shall fall out to agree with,' etc. l. 44, omit ' to' after ' from ; ' read ' the
good will of your Uncle.' l. 47, full stop after ' Ending.'
Page 7, line 6, comma after ' who.' l. 7, for ' how they must' read ' in what comeliness.'
l. 10, for ' serve' read ' assist ; ' omit ' in Peace.' l. 14, for ' Antient Machiavell' read ' Anti-
machiavill.' l. 20, for ' sure' read ' evident.' l. 25, for ' Star' read ' Share,' and ditto in next
line. l. 35, after ' that' insert ' which ; ' after ' now' insert ' so ; ' for ' argueth' read ' con-
cludeth.' l. 36, for ' of' read ' at.' l. 38, for ' Dow-Coates' read ' Dove-coate ; ' for ' old
Groundwork' read ' red groundsills.' l. 39, for ' Ancestors' read ' Ancestor.' l. 43, for
' happily' read ' he solely ; ' for ' then' read ' than.' l. 46, for ' flight Shoots' read ' Flight
Sholt.'
Page 8, line 1, full stop at ' Parentage.' l. 7, after ' Lancashire' read ' Neville of Hondry
Castle in Lancashire ; ' for ' of Strode' read ' or Strode.' l. 8, for ' Wastnes' read ' Wast-
nesse.' l. 9, for ' Elland' read ' Alland.' l. 10, after ' blood' read ' and.' l. 11, for ' thankfully' read ' thankfulness.' l. 14, after ' Vertue' insert ' The old motto belonging to your
family is, viz. *In Bivio Dextra.*' l. 15, after ' for the' insert ' better.' l. 16, for ' lend' read
' send' (see note). l. 21, for ' the Countrie' read ' their Countries.' l. 22, for ' History' read
' Historians.' l. 30, for ' Sequell and Suit' read ' Issue.' l. 39, before ' and his army' insert
' to ye Same King Edw. 3, and guided him,' etc. l. 43, for ' poulen' read ' Poulin.' l. 44,
for ' Sr Thom' read ' Sir Thomas.' l. 45, ' one hunt' ' one Hunt.'
Page 9, line 1, for ' Anno 1' ' read ' 4.' l. 6, ' facerimus' read ' fecerimus ; ' for ' ille' read
' illi ; ' for ' perdueret' read ' producerit' omitting ' nos.' l. 7, for ' nisum' read ' visum
inimicorum nostrorum.' l. 13, after ' nostram' insert ' in hoc parte adimpleri.' l. 14, for
' libris' read ' libras.' l. 15, for ' Sclacarium' read ' Saccarium.' l. 17, for ' Terra' read

---

[1] This was lost a great while, and after found again and Renewed by the same Ralph Rokeby, Penult.,
Jan. 1593, and copyed over by Thos. Rokeby of Grays Inn, anno 1654, who was afterwards Sir Thos.,
Knt., and made one of the Justices of Common Pleas in Easter Term 1st of Wm. and Mary, and afterwards one of the Justices of the Kings Bench in Michaelmas Term in the 7th year of Wm. 3rd. (This was
copied from the old MS. by Langham Rokeby, Jun., Grandfather of H. R. R., in the year 1815.)

' terræ.' l. 18, for ' facimus' read ' Fecimus.' l. 24, for ' Queen-Mother' read ' Queen's mother.' l. 26, for ' Regina' read ' Regni.' l. 32, ' and by the way,' etc., to end of line 35 ' passages.' It says, This was not in MS. l. 42, for ' Unlois' read ' Valois.' l. 44, for ' York' read ' force.'

Page 10, line 2, for ' Souch' read ' South.' l. 3, for ' Angou' read ' Angos.' l. 4, for ' Pierce' read ' Peircy.' l. 10, for ' whereupon' read ' where.' l. 15, for ' Werk' read ' York and from thence,' etc. l. 18, for ' Assigns' read ' Assizes.' l. 20, after ' holden' for ' ye same year' to line 21, ' Leaf,' read ' in ye Plea on the 27th Leaf.' l. 28, for ' Sr Henry Viscie' read ' Ursery' or ' Wassey.' l. 32, ' In Majesty' ɔmitted. l. 38, for ' needful' read ' not needful.' l. 47, for ' Wooden' read ' Tin' (MS. ' Horn ').

Page 11, line 5, ' of Majestie' omitted. l. 11, for ' Treene' read ' Tin.'[1] l. 12, ' I rather' read ' I had rather ; ' ' Treen,' ' Tin.' l. 19, for ' ye Desclation' read ' reason of ye dissolution.' l. 22, ' and his Bones . . . the Earth' omitted. ll. 23 and 24, ' and now you' omitted ; for ' Arch Peer' read ' Archpiece.' l. 25, for ' wil Humbly take our Leaves of' read ' viz. ; ' for ' peruse' read ' pursue.' l. 27, for ' Sr Ralph' read ' Sir Thos, son of Sir Thos last mentioned.' l. 28, omit ' only ; ' for ' Country' read ' County.' l. 32, for ' Country' read ' county.' l. 37, for ' worldly' read ' wily,' for ' his' read ' these.' l. 38, for ' heady' read ' hardy.' l. 39, for ' Ralph' read ' Thomas.' l. 43, after ' spolled' read ' and washed.' l. 44, omit ' to be.' l. 45, for ' he freshly' read ' they.' l. 47, for ' End and Consummation' read ' Consummation and Glory.'

Page 12, line 1, for ' Cruelly' read ' in Cruelty,' for ' in Cold Blood' read ' after the blood cooled ; ' for ' could' read ' can.' l. 2, omit ' and Unlawfull.' l. 4, after ' had' insert ' burned.' l. 7, for ' without' read ' withal.' l. 8, ' or else never' omitted. l. 11, for ' neither' read ' either.' l. 18, for ' him' read ' them.' l. 41, for ' Gro' read ' G.' l. 44, after ' English' supply ' bondage.' l. 45, for ' Capt. Rokeby, then of that peice' read ' Rokeby Capt., then of that place.'

Page 13, line 5, for ' Morton' read ' Mortham.' l. 6, ' who, etc., to Calling' omitted. l. 8, for ' Selling' read ' Fellon ; ' ' I have heard,' etc., to ' these words' wanting. l. 10, for ' Aunters' read ' Ancestors.' l. 13, for ' at' read ' that ; ' fcr ' Strange' read ' Strang.' l. 14, for ' at' read ' that ; ' for ' Lange' read ' Lang.' l. 15, for ' wheell' read ' whell ' (' quell' in margin). l. 20, for ' Yode' read ' Goed.' l. 23, ' for ' bien' read ' bren.' l. 33, for ' at' read ' that ; ' for ' Since' read ' Self.' l. 39, for ' Nusts weare' read ' at Nust or Warre ; ' ' Just or Joust.' l. 40, for ' ment' read ' men went.' l. 44, for ' fellen faire' read ' fellon fare.' l. 45, for ' fright' read ' fight.' l. 52, for ' awnters' read ' encounters.'

Page 14, line 2, for ' I' read ' they.' l. 3, after ' hole' supply ' day' viz. ' drove or driven.' l. 10, ' Reape' read ' Rope.' l. 21, for ' Brand' read ' Band.' l. 40, for ' only noked' read ' rudely rushed.' l. 42, for ' at' read ' all.' l. 48, for ' busks as' read ' bushes that.' l. 56, for ' yet walde they prayed' read ' that they would pray.'

Page 15, line 18, for ' ferd' read ' served. Stop after therefore. l. 20, for ' full' read ' for. l. 23, for ' and noy' read ' I voy' or ' vow.' l. 33, for ' at was' read ' that were.' l. 36, for ' Sike' read ' like.' l. 43, for ' force' read ' fence.' l. 49, for ' weare' read ' warre.' l. 50, for ' fast then' read ' full strong.' l. 53, for ' strange' read ' strong.' l. 57, for ' straw' read ' strave.'

Page 16, line 6, for ' band him' read ' band her him.' l. 7, for ' Kest' read ' lift.' l. 9, for ' anone he brought her' read ' they did hay.' l. 16 to end of page. These lines come in after page 15, line 29. l. 17, for ' Sichin' read ' fitchin.' l. 18, for ' out' read ' of.' l. 27, for ' deene' read ' teyne.' l. 35, for ' you' read ' yon,' ' yonder.' l. 37, for ' Zoe ghest' read ' your guest.' l. 47, for ' Namde' read ' A.' l. 48, for ' Diat' read ' Dint ; ' for ' the' read ' them.' l. 53, between this line and 54 supply ' or therefore should they die.' Last line here comes in, ' Then the letters well was made,' etc., founc at page 15, line 30, etc.

Page 17, line 25, for ' with' read ' of.' l. 29, for ' Sow Lechery' read ' Son of Lechery (' sin ' in margin). l. 32, for ' Atturney at Law' read ' apprentice of ye Common Law.' l. 33, after ' Peace' read ' and Quorum.' l. 34, after ' Daughters' read ' and co-heirs of ye house of Fitz-Harris ; ' after ' had' read ' this.' l. 35, omit ' Justice of ye Peace ; ' no full stop. l. 39, after ' issue' read ' by the daughter of Hutton of Hurwicke.' l. 40, omit ' (being 1593).' l. 41, omit the first ' William.' l. 42, omit ' had issue' supply ' Cuthbert.' l. 43, before ' Rokeby' insert ' Robert.' l. 45, after ' Robert and' insert ' Francis.' l. 46, after ' married to' insert ' Joan Rutland.' l. 50, ' wor' read ' worshipful.'

Page 18, line 1, for ' Staningford' read ' Staningforth.' l. 4, after ' friends' full stop ; ' for the,' etc. l. 6, omit ' that.' l. 8, for ' builded' read ' lived at.' l. 11, vide. l. 12, for ' Stockeld' read ' Stockell.' l. 15, after ' Auditor' read ' now owner of Staningforth, by Dorothy his wife, the Dr of Gascoigne of Caley, hath issue.' l. 16, after ' Anthony' read ' his eldest son (married to Jane, Dr of Wm Sutton of Aram, by whom he hath issue Henry, an infant of tender years, whom G. grant not to see any the like calamities of England), and Thomas his 2nd son, a young man of good hope, and William Rokeby, and 2 daughters, Jane and Elizabeth. Jane, the Dr of James R. of Staningforth, was married to Wm Stavely of Stavely, near Ripon, by whom she hath issue, now living, Sampson, Thomas, Ann, Ursula, Dorothy, and Elizabeth. Sampson Stavely married the Dr of Wm Lister, Kt. l. 19, Anthony Rokeby, eldest son of Jas Rokeby of Staningforth, had in marriage for his 2nd wife. l. 20, Mary, ye Dr of Geo. Abney of Wilsley, near Ashby-de-la-Zouch, and by her had issue five sons. l. 21,

' Treen' is the correct reading, meaning ' wooden.'

George, James, Thomas, Fulke, and Anthony, and five D^rs, Frances, Margaret, Elizabeth, Anne, and Elinor. l. 23, George Rokeby, citizen of London, the eldest son of Anthony by the 2nd wife, married the D^r of Robert Underwood in Hertfordshire, by whom he hath Issue six sons, John, James, George, Ralph, Thomas, and William. l. 25, and three daughters, viz., Grace married to Mr Wm Drinkwater, citizen of London, Rhode married to Mr Boylston of Leitchfield, and Sarah married to one Mr Field, a citizen of London. ll. 26 to 29 not in my copy. l. 30, Thomas ye 3^d son of Anthony (2nd son omitted), Rector of Warmsworth, married Ann the 2nd D^r of Gervase Lea of Norwell, Esqr., and by her hath issue Thomas, William, and Gervase. ll. 31 to 44, not in my copy. l 45, Fulke Rokeby, ye 4th son, married ye D^r of John King, Bishop of Elgin, in the County of Westmeath in Ireland.

Page 19, line 1, 'Anthony, ye 5th Son, married the D^r of Mr Grundy of Thorgarten, in the County of Nottingham. l. 14, for 'Stanningforth' read 'Staningforth.' l. 20, 'of Morton' omitted. l. 25, 'Gulielmus 2nd Filius, Johannes 3^tius Filius.' l. 26, after 'et' supply 'hæres Gulielme;' 'Thomas, 4^tus filius. l. 28, for 'patris' read 'patri.' l. 29, no stop after 'Hart-hill.' l. 34, after 'the 4th' supply 'and youngest.' l. 38, for 'about a Wainscot' read 'in a Wainscott Stall.'

Page 20, line 5, after 'if you' read 'sh^d prove nought worthy ye name of.' l. 9, nothing in my copy after 'Friends' till line 30. l. 15, before 'I wonder' insert 'Fierce foe fierce fiend thy ravening jaws why opest why grinnest' (W.). l. 32, for 'by use' read 'with an use.' l. 35, for 'Saxley' read 'Saxby.' l. 46, for 'the whole' read 'the wilde.' l. 47, for 'Men' read 'Livers.' l. 50, for 'Arch bishop' read 'Bishop.'

Page 21, line 2, for 'Rickald' here and in line 3 read 'Record. l. 20, for 'an Hundred' read 'two men.' l. 23, omit 'they.' l. 27, omit 'yet.' l. 33, for 'Bandioca,' etc., read 'Bandiosa Vechia honor de Capitano.' l. 34, 'for a Tenth warr' read 'a tent of war.' l. 36, for 'the Stow' read 'the Store.' l. 37, for 'Constable, a daughter' read 'Constable's D^r.' l. 41, 'of Thornton' read 'of Thornton Watlas and Headlam.' l. 43, for 'Brackenbrough' read 'Brackenburgh's D^r.' l. 46, after 'by' read 'ye D^r of Thweng Sir Thos Rokeby.' l. 47, supply 'who by Sir Ralph Lawson's D^r of Drough.' l. 48, for 'these Brethren' read 'those six brothers;' after 'Jo: Rokeby' supply 'who by my fashion and by S^t a maukin (for these were his usual Phrases of speaking).'

Page 22, line 1, for 'Cannon' read 'Common.' l. 9, for 'Jonston' read 'Tueston. l. 28, after 'had of' supply 'him.' l. 29, for 'bounden knowledge' read 'with bounden thanks acknowledge.' l. 32, 'for 'Melton' read 'Molton.' l. 33, for 'Mackenworth' read 'Mackworth.'

Page 23, line 20, for 'casting' read 'cassing.' l. 26, for 'the Father' read 'your Father.' l. 36, for 'the following' read 'this memorial in.' l. 38, for 'Then' read 'The;' for 'evills foe' read 'ill man's foe.'

Page 24, line 1, 'Philip and Mary' no stop. l. 14, for 'against Rebells' read 'for his Prince against Rebels.' l. 15, for 'Service' read 'Circuit.' l. 20, for 'Markham' read 'Marsham.' l. 44, 'Paris, Estampes, Fearille, Casteau, Dreux, Vendosia, Allenton, Mantes and Falaise.'

Page 25, l. 2, for 'present and first arrived' read 'presence and first arrival.' l. 3, for 'of Diep' read 'at Dieppe.' l. 6, for 'Basceruito' read 'Basterville.' l. 10, 'bud out' should be 'budded out of your chins.' l. 13, after 'Stubbs' read 'buried in.' l. 17, for 'Civill piety' read 'singular' and 'admirable civil virtues.' l. 26, for 'lowly' read 'loving.' l. 32, 'jugalis' should be 'jugali.' l. 34, 'æqualis' should be 'æquates.' l. 39, for 'animi' read 'mulier.' l. 41, for 'cederet' read 'rederet a vita;' for 'parvit' read 'paruit.' l. 42 should be 'paruit, et tenebras.' l. 44, for 'Suspira' read 'suspiria.' l. 46, for 'Flore' read 'flere,' and for 'vetat' read 'requit.' l. 49, for 'Egerit' read 'Egent.' l. 50, for 'que major' read 'quæ nelior.'

Page 26, line 5 should be 'Dulce decus que merim.' l. 11, for 'Superas' read 'Superis;' for 'audire' read 'adire domos.' l. 12, for 'chare' read 'chara.' l. 14, for 'illus' read 'illuc.' l. 19, for 'est' read 'en.' l. 32 should be 'atque tuam fer opim mihi dura cuventi.' l. 33, should be 'r' ovas εκ δίδι εστι.' l. 35, for 'Equalis' read 'Æquales.' l. 37, for 'Soluti' read 'secutil.' l. 38, for 'auditum' read 'aditum.' l. 44, for 'his' read 'hic.' l. 46, for 'volens' read 'volans.' l. 47, after 'Docuit' supply 'docuit post,' etc. l. 52, for 'Illis' read 'illi;' no 'Uxor' after 'creandis.' l. 53, line omitted, 'Uxor certo operam, doctæ haud ignara Minervæ.

Page 27, line 2, after 'Succedant' read 'illus feliciter, illis.' l. 8 should begin 'Uxoris verus sit.' l. 9, for 'Est' read 'atque.' l. 10, for 'alma Venus' read 'Venus alma.' l. 12 should begin 'O certo precor, O Rokebeus.' l. 13, for 'plaudo' read 'placido.' l. 15, 'Exuperat' read 'famæque.' l. 16, 'generosa.' l. 18, 'Læto' should be 'læta.' l. 22, for 'Skerbrough' read 'Skorbrough n^r Beverley,' supply 'and left him 3 sons viz. Ch^s Hotham, sometime fellow of Peterhouse in Cambridge, and Durand and Wm Hotham.' l. 31, for 'Westly' read 'Westby.' l. 32, after 'Uncle' supply '(Thos R. of Morton) and 2 Drs Margaret and Faith.' l. 34, for 'Phillips' read 'Phillis.' l. 35, for 'afternamed' read 'fore-named.' l. 39, for 'Thornesby' read 'Thornby.' l. 45, for 'unto' read 'under.' l. 46, for 'and Captain' read 'and last at Norram Chase.'

Page 28, lines 4 and 5, from 'Ralph Rokeby' to 'married' is omitted. My copy reads thus:—'Ralph R. ye 2nd son apprentice at law,' etc. l. 12, for 'first' read 'one of ye first.' l. 33, after 'Virtue' supply 'Eliz. was after married to Mr Richard Vincent of Firsby, and

Susan to M[r] W[m] Cartwright of Normandy in Lincolnshire.' l. 36, ' one Daughter Mary married to Christopher Legard.' L. 39, married ' Frances.' L 41, after ' William ' supply ' who died without issue on 24th yr of his age ;' ' Alexander married to Margaret, D[r] of Jo Cooke of Holkham in Norfolk, Esq.'; ' Willoughby, now of Lincolns Inn.' l. 42, ' Francis, who died in France about 20th yr of his age ;' for ' 2 Daughters ' read ' 4, Mary, Elizabeth, Mildred, and Bridgett. He had many more children but they died young,' L 44, for ' Warmsworth ' read ' Edlington.' l. 45, after ' Wiliam ' read ' now of Sandal ;' after ' Alexander ' read ' who died at Trinity Coll. in Cambridge about the 17th yr of his age ' omitting ' a sweet babes ' to ' Blessings.'

Page 29, line 2, for ' places,' etc., read ' remembrances of,' etc. l. 4, ' Suit of Time ' read ' ye tracke of time ;' ' The place where of greatest,' etc. l. 11, for ' parties ' read ' persons ;' omit ' or at least in those habits.' L 16, ' for ' Dissolution ' read ' Dissoluteness.' l. 19, after ' them ' read ' for Vengeance ;' ' for Sin ' omitted. l. 22, for ' I am ' read ' Jam.' l. 28, for ' Conventicle ' read ' Convent.' l. 36, for ' Coal ' read ' Coat.' L 41, ' was Steward ;' omit ' his.' l. 42, for ' Testimony ' read ' Testament.'

Page 30, line 13, for ' a Bear baitings ' read ' the Bearbaits.' L 24,' Syncliff Grange.' l. 25, for ' Askew ' read ' Aschough.' l. 28, for ' Chaulthorpes ' read ' Calthorpe.' l. 29, for ' we ' read ' me.' l. 47, for ' Lewd ' read ' Loud.' L 48, for ' Ale Hunters ' read ' Hall-haunters.'

Page 31, line 2, for ' of ' read ' with.' l. 3, for ' others ' read ' other.' l. 24, for ' donius ' read ' domus.' l. 29, for ' Cresces ' read ' cresce.' l. 30, for ' pomo feras ' read ' poma ferat.' l. 40, for ' S[t] John de Nelsars ' read ' S[r] Joh de Melsas.' L 41, ' of Bener ' read ' of Benekt.' L 44, for ' Wighell ' read ' Weighill.'

Page 32, from No. 14, ' Christopher, and not from 13, is descended the House of Hotham ; No. 17, ' Fawcetts D[r] Citizen of London ;' No. 18, Tho[s] Rokeby Esq[r] to ye D[r] of Wicliff of Gales.'

NOTES.

Page 7, line 13, As for that Arch Atheist Nicholas Machiavill I trust my Co[zns] will not look on him, but if you do read after this Frenchman you shall see an Ass pointed out by his Ears and painted in as lively colours as ever Apelles painted Alexander, Polignotus, ye captive ladies, Zeuxis his grapes, yea or any of them any of their works. I mean not his works of the history of Florence, nor of the art of war, for they are good, but his discourses of Livy and his principles are to make of men devills in carnate. l. 16, ' and this rank,' etc. The MS. on parchment begins here. L 40, ' Morton ;' in margin it says ' Mortham.' l. 41, ' or else ' to l. 44 ' liking ' not in MS.

Page 8, line 1, I note here only your Blood and Coat-armes descended unto you, and not such as y[r] Ancestors have impayled by their marriages. l. 16, from ' lest haply ' to L 19 ' besprinkle y[r] child[n]' omitted in MS.

Page 9, line 1. This is verified by this sent unto me by my good friend M[r] Michael Henage Keeper of the records in ye Tower (apparently added by Tho[s] Rokeby the judge). l. 20, This is inserted by Tho[s] Rokeby 2, but was not in MS. : ' I have a patent from Edw 3, dated at Reading the 4th of Nov[r] in the 5th yr of his reign, wherein he recites the former patent whereby he had given the s[d] Thomas de R £100 p[r] ann out of the Exchequer, and in consider[n] of his release of that grants him the sum of £253, 6s. 8d. out of the Exchequer, and also the Manor of Paulinsgray in the County of Kent wh was £17, 3s. 8d. p ann and lands in Green Hamerton in Yorksh wh were 6s. 8d. p ann wh were the lands of Michael de Hartley forfeited to the King and lands at Rabergh in Westmoreland worth 7s. p ann wh were the lands of Andr de Hartley forfeited likewise and many other lands therementioned, wh patent I bought of one Washington (whose living it is to sell Antiquities and unprinted reports) Jan 1st 1659. About the 12th and 13 of Edw 3 Tho[s] de Rokeby was Governor of the Castles of Barwick, Edenburgh and Sterling as appears by the Rolls of ye Parl[t] held in Octobis Hillarii 13 Edw 3 4th Pt Sover[n] Power of Parliament page 5. In an old Coucher Bk of ye Dean and Chapter of York called Doomesday Bk (fol 16) Henry de Rokeby is one of the Jurers (the Jury being made up of Knights and Gentlemen) to enquire of liberties between the Mayor of York and the Dean and Chapter Anno 7th Edw 1st Ann Dom 1275.'

Page 10, line 5, note, ' My good friend M[r] Mich Heanage of the Tower Office sent me a note of a Chron dated 20th of Edw 3 wherein Sir Tho[s] Rokeby Statū Banoretti suscepit in obsidio Regis Scoti Anno 20 Edw 3 M 21.' L 29, ' You must forth,' etc., to l. 32, ' Kings grant,' not in MS.

Page 11, line 18, Died at the Castle of Kilka in Ireland in 25th of Edw 3rd after he had been 6 years Justiciary of Ireland.—Vide History of York. l. 27, Mattin's Hist., vol. i. p. 174 ; Kennett's Coll., vol. iii. p. 297 ; De Rapin Thoyras, tom. iii. p. 403, call him Sir Thomas Rokeby. l. 33, after ' Northumberland,' ' and ye Ld Burdolf and sent both their Heads to London, where they were fixed on poles on the Bridge.' These words are in my copy with a note, not in MS.

Page 12, line 12, from ' name him ' to l. 30 ' diligence' omitted, but L 25, ' of whom,' etc., to ' diligence,' l. 30, seems to have been in MS., from note in margin.

Page 13, line 39, in margin, ' just ' or jousting, tournament.

Page 15, line 29, between this line and the next are the following lines :—

' We gave her battle half a day
and fitchis was fain to fly away
for saving of our life
And Pater Dale wd never blinn
but as fast as he cd rinn, till he came to his wife
The warden sd I am full woe
That ever ye shd be torment soe, but had we with you been
Had we been there your brethren all
We shd have garred the warle fall, that wrought you all this teyn
Fryer Middleton said Soone pay
in faith you wd have fled away, when most Mister had beene.'

Page 21, line 7, Agnes the 2nd Dr was married to James Strangwayes. Alice was married to John Aeklam and all these and Roger Lascelles ; Sir Richd Strangwayes and Elizabeth married to Wm Balmer were cousins and coheirs to Sir Rd Conyers of Lands and Blood, appearing by a Deed of Partition dated the 7th Henry and remaining in my cousin James Strangwayes hands whereof I have a copy. l. 18, Christopher Rokeby was then wounded with 5 or 6 wounds and his servant Bainbridge killed at his foot who ran betwixt his Master and Death. l. 46, This Thos had issue Francis who succeeded him at Morton and by Faucetts Dr of London hath issue 2 Sons and 3 Drs.

Page 22, line 5, ' Plato.'

Page 23, line 15, He chose this Thos to be his Lieuts but the Ld Hunsclo the Ld Chamberlain and Govr of Barwich thrust another to him to be His Lieut and he not willing to displease the gt Ld nor displace his kinsman (an apt and brave companion of arms) took them both to be his Lieuts taking from his own pay to supply them ; which made Thos R to contend in extreme toil, so that his Fellow gave over in Service, and in gt heat putting off a heavy plated coate and putting on a coarse canvas dublitt all full of holes it melted his grease and this he told me himself on his Death-bed. l. 29, This seems a mistake, for Morgan was Chief-Justice of the Common Pleas, and not of the King's Bench. l. 34, Sir Wm Cordell was Speaker of the House of Commons in the 1st yr of Phil and Mary.

Page 24, line 36, ' Dorothy' married afterwards to Wm Rokeby of Hotham, my Grandfather. l. 41, This Thomas by his wife had issue Grace his only Dr and Heir married to Conyers, Ld Darcy and Conyers.

Page 25, line 16, Wm Lambert made the Bk of the Saxon laws, ye Justice of Peace, ye perambulation of Kent, a book of the original of Courts unprinted, and endowed the fair Hospital of Greenwich, and had his right hand cut off for writing agst the Qu Elizs marriage with Anjou.—Baker, 520.

Page 27, line 19, She giveth me also £150 pr ann. I thank her and her late husband Michael Warton, therefore. l. 32, ' Thomas.' This Thos married one Mrs. Smith of Beverley, and had issue by her Thos Rokeby Knt and Marshal de Camp in France.

Page 28, L 4, This Ralph was he that made ye Ld Chancellor Egerton his executor wh was worth near £10,000 to the Ld Chancellor. Bottom of page (half a page blank). Supply :—

Thos R of Barnby 3rd son married Eliz. Dr of Wm Bury of Grantham in Lincolnsh. Esqr and by her had issue (1) Wm R now of Burnby[1] (who married Emma the Dr of Wm Bury of Grantham and by her hath issue one Dr named Emm) (2) Thomas sometime fellow of Katherine Hall in Camb. and now of Grays Inn, (3) John R, now a factor in the W. Indies (4) Jos R and (5) Benjn R and 6 Drs (1) Eliz. died unmarried about the 19th yr of her age (2) Mary, (3) Emm, (4) Ann, (5) Susan and (6) Dorothy who died in the 3rd year of her age.

Philip R ye 4th son of Wm R of Hotham married Jane the Dr of Wm Godfrey of Humnock in Lincolnsh Esqr and by her had issue 3 sons viz. Joseph Philip and Nathaniel and 1 Dr Katherine, Benjn R married Rebekah Dr and Heiress of Thos Langham of Arthingworth, Northamptonsh by whom he had Langham Rokeby and 2 Drs Rebekah and Elizabeth.

Langham Rokeby of Arthth married Catherine ye Dr of Major Nicolaus Morgan and by her had Langham R, Thomas and Elizabeth. Langham died in his infancy, Eliz. died unmarried.

Thos R married Eliz. Scott ye only Dr of Col. John Scott of Galashield in the County of Teviotsdale, North Britain, upon wh marriage the following copy of Verses were made by Mrs Eliza Tollitt—

Mrs Eliza Tollitts Verses on the Marriage of Thos Rokeby with Eliz. Dr of Col. Scott.

Invisible and unconfined by place
Yr rural haunts the Heaven-born Muse can trace
Where smiling Love attends the beauteous Bride
And the calm hours in Golden circles glide—
Remote from tumult Avarice and Pride

[1] Slain at Dunbar, Sep. 3, 1650.

Her airy steps pursue where'er you rove
Ascend the Hill and range around the grove
Where thro' the Sylvan glade her view she tires
To count the Distant Hills and rising Spires
Where the 1ˢᵗ object that yr eyes command
Thro' Vistas planted by a Fathers hand [1]
Is the fair prospect of Paternal land
For wealth let others try the faithless main
More certain are the labours of the swain
For you this verdure springs, this harvest grows
And these tall oaks their spacious arches close.
Or now reposing in the Rustic Cell [2]
Or in the Bowers of lovely Philomel [2]
Yr own Soft voice assists the lovers string
And all the woods with gay Vertummis ring
All shapes to please ye Amorous youth had tried
But with his own the Captive Nymph complied
So may thyself be blest and so thy grove
Where conscious virtue dwells and constant Love.

Page 29, line 23, 'colunt.' I mean they till and plough them, not that they worship them.

[1] Sunderland Wood planted by I. R., belonging to the property at Arthingworth.
[2] Places in the wood called by these names.

— ———————— .

INDEX OF NAMES.

N.B.—*This Index does not include the names in Appendices and Notes, or the members of the Rokeby family.*

e